NO BODY

Fargo examined the tracks more carefully. Instead of the rounded edge of a boot or shoe at the front of each, there were five slight indentations. They looked, for all the world, like claw marks. But he was absolutely certain the figure had been a man.

"What the hell?" Fargo said out loud. Scratching his chin, he looked about for more prints.

There were only the two under the overhang. The rest had been obliterated by the storm.

Puzzled, Fargo shoved the Henry into the scabbard, forked leather, and resumed his journey. He had a few miles to go to the inn.

He reached the main trail and reined to the south, thinking of the meal he would treat himself to. Beefsteak with all the trimmings sounded nice. And a gallon of coffee to wash the food down.

The next moment his empty belly became the least of his concerns.

For there, lying in the middle of the trail, was a human head.

THE TRAILSMAN
#391

NIGHT TERROR

by

Jon Sharpe

A SIGNET BOOK

SIGNET
Published by the Penguin Group
Penguin Group (USA) LLC, 375 Hudson Street,
New York, New York 10014

USA I Canada I UK I Ireland I Australia I New Zealand I India I South Africa I China
penguin.com
A Penguin Random House Company

First published by Signet, an imprint of New American Library,
a division of Penguin Group (USA) LLC

First Printing, May 2014

The first chapter of this book previously appeared in *Devil's Den*, the three hundred
ninetieth volume in this series.

℗ REGISTERED TRADEMARK—MARCA REGISTRADA

ISBN 978-0-451-46802-4

Printed in the United States of America
10 9 8 7 6 5 4 3 2 1

The Trailsman

Beginnings . . . they bend the tree and they mark the man. Skye Fargo was born when he was eighteen. Terror was his midwife, vengeance his first cry. Killing spawned Skye Fargo, ruthless, cold-blooded murder. Out of the acrid smoke of gunpowder still hanging in the air, he rose, cried out a promise never forgotten.

The Trailsman, they began to call him all across the West: searcher, scout, hunter, the man who could see where others only looked, his skills for hire but not his soul, the man who lived each day to the fullest, yet trailed each tomorrow. Skye Fargo, the Trailsman, the seeker who could take the wildness of a land and the wanting of a woman and make them his own.

*1861, the Arkansas swamp country—and
the winds of war are in the air.*

1

The thunderstorm threatened to catch Skye Fargo in the open. He'd hoped to reach the inn he was bound for before it broke but the front moved too swiftly. The afternoon sky was dark with roiling clouds. Shrieking wind bent the trees and the already humid air was heavy with the promise of the rain to come.

Fargo needed to seek cover. Arkansas storms could be gully washers. He wasn't partial to the notion of having his hat and buckskins soaked clean through. So when he came to a bend and spied a smaller trail leading off into the woods, he reined into it, thinking it might take him to a settler's cabin where he could ask to be put up until the storm passed. Some home cooking wouldn't hurt, either. He had money in his poke to pay for a meal.

The wind keened louder and the trees whipped in a frenzy. In the distance thunder rumbled.

Fargo went around a bend and drew rein in mild surprise. He'd found a cabin, all right, but it had seen better days. Half the roof had buckled, the front door lay on the ground, and vines hung over the window. Still, it was shelter. Dismounting, he held firm to the reins and led the Ovaro around to the side where an overhang jutted four or five feet. It would protect the stallion from the worst of the rain. Patting the Ovaro's neck, he said, "This will have to do, big fella."

The Ovaro stamped a hoof. It wasn't skittish like some horses were with thunder and lightning, unless the storm was severe.

Fargo tied the reins, shucked his Henry rifle from the saddle scabbard, and went around to the front doorway and peered in. There was a dank odor. Warily entering, he kicked the wall to test how sturdy it was. Then, squatting, he faced the doorway and placed the Henry across his lap.

Fargo's stomach growled, reminding him he hadn't eaten all day. There was pemmican in his saddlebags. He should have helped himself to a few pieces but now it would have to wait.

With a tremendous thunderclap, Nature unleashed her elemental fury. A deluge fell, rain so heavy that Fargo couldn't see three feet, the drops so large that they struck the ground like hail. He heard the Ovaro whinny and glanced through a gap in the wall. The stallion had its head high and its ears pricked but it wasn't trying to break free.

The downpour continued. Lightning seared the firmament again and again. A particularly vivid bolt seemed to light up the entire sky and lent an eerie glow to the falling rain. The glow faded, but before it did, Fargo could have sworn he saw something silhouetted against the backdrop of the trees, something on two legs, and huge.

Fargo's first thought was that it must be a bear. There weren't any grizzlies in Arkansas but there were plenty of black bears and some of them grew to considerable size. It might be seeking shelter from the rain, too.

Fargo rose and levered a round into the Henry's chamber. The last thing he wanted was to tangle with a bruin. He waited but nothing appeared. He was about convinced he must have imagined it when another bolt turned the rain into a shimmering waterfall, and there, barely a long stride from the doorway, stood the great hulking figure he had seen before.

Involuntarily, Fargo's breath caught in his throat. He couldn't make much out. It was a man—that was certain—taller than he was and twice as wide across the shoulders. A man wearing a hooded affair that draped practically to his knees. In the flash from the lightning, the man's entire body seemed to blaze with fire. Then the light faded, and Fargo cleared his throat and said, "Who's there?"

There was no answer.

Fargo stepped to the doorway. Cold drops spattered his cheeks and brow as he hollered again, "Who's there? You're welcome to join me." He said that even though part of him sensed an indefinable danger.

Again there was no reply.

Fargo glanced at the Ovaro to be sure it was still there. He faced the doorway as a sound wafted out of the storm, a ululating howl that rose from a low pitch to a high wail. Goose bumps erupted as he realized it must have come from the throat of the man he had just seen and not from any animal. Taking a step back, he leveled the Henry. He half expected the apparition to charge out of the downpour but the howl faded and nothing happened.

Fargo stayed standing a long while. Finally he eased down cross-legged and tried to make sense of the giant shape and the eerie cry. He was amid low hills at the edge of bayou country. The locals were a mix of backwoodsmen and denizens of the deep swamps. Poor folks, mostly. They weren't always friendly to strangers but by and large they were hospitable enough.

They weren't known for howling in rainstorms.

Maybe the man was drunk. He recollected that time in Denver when he'd had so much whiskey that when he walked a dove to her boardinghouse, he'd howled at the moon to amuse her.

He listened for another but the rain and the thunder went on unbroken. For over an hour the tempest lashed the earth. At last the rain slackened and the thunder faded and the darkness brightened to gray.

Fargo stayed put until no drops fell. Stepping outside, he admired the wet world the storm had left in its wake: the glistening leaves and dripping limbs, the sheen on the grass, the blue pools and here and there a tiny rivulet.

Going to the overhang, Fargo was about to unwrap the Ovaro's reins when he drew up short. Etched in the dirt were a pair of tracks. Footprints, easily the largest he'd ever seen. He placed his own boot next to one and whistled. The other was at least four inches longer and half again as wide. The man was a giant. Fargo was glad he hadn't tried to take the stallion.

Set to climb on, Fargo froze a second time. Squatting, he examined the tracks more carefully. Instead of the rounded edge of a boot or shoe at the front of each, there were five slight indentations. They looked, for all the world, like claw marks. But he was absolutely certain the figure had been a man.

"What the hell?" Fargo said out loud. Scratching his chin, he looked about for more prints.

There were only the two under the overhang. The rest had been obliterated by the storm.

Puzzled, Fargo shoved the Henry into the scabbard, forked leather, and resumed his journey. He had a few miles to go to the inn. It had taken him two days more to reach Arkansas than the army counted on but he'd had a far piece to come.

He reached the main trail and reined to the south, thinking of the meal he would treat himself to. Beefsteak with all the trimmings sounded nice. And a gallon of coffee to wash the food down.

The next moment his empty belly became the least of his concerns.

For there, lying in the middle of the trail, was a human head.

2

In hostile country west of the Mississippi River it was rare but not unusual to come on atrocities. A family of homesteaders, butchered. Emigrants with a wagon train, wiped out. But this was Arkansas. There were no hostiles. Outlaws, yes, but none that Fargo heard of went around chopping off heads.

Drawing rein, Fargo stared in disbelief. The head was that of a young man with sandy hair and beard and with eyes almost as blue as Fargo's own. Ragged strips of flesh told Fargo the head hadn't been chopped off. It had been ripped from the neck with incredible brute strength.

Then Fargo noticed something else. Something that gave him a start and made him place his hand on his Colt.

The head was dry.

It had been placed there *after* the storm.

With a flick of his wrist, Fargo drew. He scanned the vegetation to the right and left of the trail but saw no one.

Scuttling clouds still filled much of the sky and the woods were in shadow. The man—or thing—that did this could be anywhere.

Dismounting, Fargo debated. He could kick the head into the brush or bury it. Except that the local law would want to know of the murder, and to see the grisly find for themselves.

Fargo wasn't about to carry it. He decided to wrap it in a blanket. Untying his bedroll, he was hunkering to unroll it when the undergrowth moved more than the fading wind would cause.

Gliding to an oak, Fargo crouched. "Who's there?" he called out. "I know someone is."

No one replied.

Fargo had no intention of going in after them. As wet as everything was, the killer could stalk him silently. Wet twigs didn't snap like dry ones. Wet grass didn't crunch underfoot.

Time crawled.

Fargo held himself still, waiting for the other man to give himself away. When he had to, he could be as patient as an Apache.

4

He'd outwait whoever it was. They were bound to make a mistake eventually.

Suddenly Fargo sensed that he wasn't alone. Every instinct he possessed warned that someone had crept up behind him. He began to whirl and glimpsed—something—out of the corner of his eye.

And then the back of his skull caved in.

Consciousness returned slowly in fitful spikes of feeling that filled him with pain and then drowned him in waves of darkness. Each spike lasted longer, until, with a gasp and a jolt, he opened his eyes and sat up. He shouldn't have. Agony was the only way to describe his head. He raised a hand and discovered a knot. That, and his hair matted by dried blood.

Fargo realized that if whoever struck him had done so any harder, he wouldn't be breathing. He had been lucky. Nausea struck, and he doubled over and breathed deeply until the sickening sensation stopped.

Only then did he remember the head.

It was still there, in the middle of the trail. Only now it wore a hat. *His* hat, once white but now brown from so much use.

"Son of a bitch," Fargo exclaimed. Whoever slugged him had done it just to put his hat on the severed head? That was plain loco. It was the sort of senseless prank a child might play.

Fargo snatched his hat, swiped at some blood, and placed it back on. It made his head hurt worse.

"Thanks for the warning," he said to the Ovaro. It was a wonder the stallion hadn't been taken. Most highwaymen wouldn't pass up a fine mount. Then again, most highwaymen didn't rip heads off.

Fargo wasted no more time. He wrapped the head in a blanket, cut whangs from his sleeves to fashion a long cord, and wrapped the cord around the bundle so the head wouldn't fall out. Since the head wouldn't fit in a saddlebag, he hung it from his saddle horn.

As he stepped into the stirrups, his instincts screamed another warning. Unseen eyes were on him. He looked but saw only forest.

His head pounding, he lightly tapped his spurs to the Ovaro. The squish of hooves, the slap of mud drowned out any other sounds. He came to a bend and slowed to look back.

Off in the trees a huge form flitted. It was there and it was gone, so fleeting that had he blinked, he'd have missed it. Like before, he couldn't make out much other than the thing was immense.

"I owe you, you son of a bitch," Fargo said.

Was he hearing things, or did it answer in a low grunt?

Fargo rode on. He became aware of being shadowed. He never saw anyone but he could sense a presence. The shadow's woodcraft was superb. Whoever it was could move like a ghost. The shadowing went on for miles.

If not for the menace, Fargo would have enjoyed himself. The Arkansas woods were lush with life. Songbirds warbled, a jay squawked, a cardinal lent a splash of red to the green.

His shadow finally left him. As if it wanted him to know, it made a lot of noise moving off. And then something occurred that made Fargo wonder if he was wrong about it being a man.

The thing roared.

3

Fargo had never been to the Havenpeak Inn. The name gave the impression it must be on a mountain but the inn sat on a hill. A high hill by Arkansas standards, but at two hundred feet it was a bump compared to the Rockies.

The inn was built in colonial times by a shipping magnate who wanted a quiet place to get away. It drew so many visitors that a small hamlet, called Haven, sprang up at the bottom of the hill.

That was all the background the army had given Fargo, and now here he was, near the end of his long ride from Fort Laramie.

Fargo hadn't liked being asked to deliver a pouch. He was a scout, not a dispatch rider, but the army needed someone they were confident could get through to General Canton. He had no idea what was in the pouch. The colonel at Fort Laramie hinted it had something to do with the rumor that a war between the North and the South might break out sometime soon.

All Fargo wanted was to deliver it and head back.

Havenpeak was an impressive stone-and-lumber edifice. A gravel road wound up it past outbuildings and shacks and a stable. It seemed strange to see well-dressed patrons casually strolling about the well-maintained gardens in the middle of the Arkansas wilderness.

Fargo drew rein at the stable and dismounted. He would love nothing better than to take the dispatch pouch and his saddlebags and go wash up but first things first.

A stableman in an outfit that looked more fitting for winter wear than summer came up the aisle and bowed his head. "Sir, I'll see to your horse if you don't mind."

"Who's in charge here?" Fargo asked.

"Sir?"

"The inn," Fargo clarified. "Who runs it?"

"Mr. Lafferty owns it but he's hardly ever here. Mr. Hoffstedder, the manager, is the gentleman to see."

"I'd be obliged if you'd fetch him."

The stableman hesitated. "I don't mind doing so, sir. I don't mind

7

at all. But you see, Mr. Hoffstedder doesn't like to be disturbed unless it's important. Are you sure someone else can't help you?"

Fargo took the bundle off his saddle horn, set it down, and opened the blanket enough for the stableman to see what it contained. "What do you think? Is this important enough?"

The whites of the stableman's eyes showed as he took a step back and exclaimed, "Land sakes! Another one! I'll fetch Mr. Hoffstedder right quick."

"Don't tell him why."

"Sir?"

"Just say I'd like to see him," Fargo said. The army wanted him to avoid attracting attention, as the colonel put it, to keep his mission secret from "the other side."

"Very well, sir."

While he waited, Fargo stripped the Ovaro, placed his saddle and saddle blanket in the tack room, and put the stallion in a stall. He was feeding it oats when the stableman hurried in with another man puffing behind him.

"This is Mr. Hoffstedder, sir."

The manager wasn't much over five feet tall and nearly as wide. He had on a knee-length coat and a top hat and carried a cane with a brass knob. "I trust this is important. My man, Eli, here, informs me that you insisted on seeing me and that it's urgent but he wouldn't say why."

Fargo unwrapped his bundle a second time.

Hoffstedder paled and took a step back, his hand rising to his throat. "God in heaven. Is there no end?"

"To what?" Fargo asked.

"To these killings," Hoffstedder replied without taking his eyes off the grisly find. "To the horror of murder after murder." He extended his cane and touched the head and it rolled over, facing him. "My word! I know that fellow. It's Jerrod Wilkes. His family has lived here a good many years."

"Who would want to kill him?"

Instead of answering, Hoffstedder wheeled and lumbered from the stable as fast as his feet could take him. "Don't go anywhere. I'll be back with the sheriff in no time," he said over his shoulder.

Fargo wouldn't have thought there was a lawman within a hundred miles. "Sheriff?" he said to Eli.

"Yes, sir. Sheriff Ashley. He came from the county seat about two months ago because of the first killing and he's been staying down to Haven ever since."

"How many dead have they found?"

The whites of Eli's eyes were showing once more. "It's only ever the heads, sir. Never a body to go with them."

"I'll be damned."

"Like that," Eli said, with a bob of his chin. "Seven so far, I do believe. They always show up in the strangest places. The first was found in the middle of a street in Haven. The second was jammed on a rake in front of the general store. Another one was placed on the steps of the church." Eli lowered his voice. "Folks says as how there's a haunt on the loose. They call it the Night Terror."

"A ghost that rips off heads?" Fargo said, and couldn't resist a grin.

"*Something* is doing it, sir," Eli said. "And if it's not a spook, then you tell me what goes around ripping off heads?"

Fargo thought of the giant figure in the rain. "Has anyone ever seen this spook of yours?"

"A few folks," Eli said. "They say it's real big and moves like a ghost and vanishes into thin air."

"Don't believe everything you hear," Fargo said.

"Then there're the tracks," Eli went on. "Folks have been whispering they ain't entirely human."

"I've seen a few," Fargo said, "and they were strange."

"There you go, sir," Eli said. He looked around and lowered his voice. "Although there're also those as say it's not no spook but a monster."

"Oh brother," Fargo said.

"They say it comes out of the swamp at night to tear off heads and then goes back into the swamp to sleep the days away."

"It's nice to know they have it figured out."

"What do you think is doing it, sir?"

"An idiot." Fargo's stomach growled again, reminding him of how famished he was. "If anyone wants me, I'll be in the inn."

"But Mr. Hoffstedder told us to wait here."

"He's your boss, not mine." Fargo adjusted the strap to the dispatch pouch, which was slanted across his chest.

"He'll be powerful mad you didn't listen."

"I'm plumb scared." Fargo draped his saddlebags over his shoulder, rested the Henry in the crook of an arm, and grinned. "Don't let the Night Terror get you."

"Oh, sir," Eli said, but he grinned. "You're the one who should worry. The Night Terror only kills white folks."

"It had its chance and left my head on."

9

Hoffstedder must have said something to others. Word was spreading and strollers from the garden were converging and people were coming out of the inn.

Over a dozen so far, including several women in gay dresses and hats and one with a parasol.

Fargo drew a lot of stares as he shouldered through them. His boots scuffed the marble steps and then he was in a cool foyer with hardwood walls and a polished floor and a grandfather clock ticking away. He didn't cross to the front desk. Instead, he turned under a wide arch and took a seat at a table. Almost immediately a waiter appeared, bearing a menu.

"Don't people eat around here?" Fargo said as he leaned the Henry against a chair. No one else was there.

The waiter, a gray-haired gent with rheumy eyes, gestured at tables with plates of half-eaten food. "Everyone has gone to see the head, sir." He paused. "Do you know about them?"

"I'm learning." Fargo said. He opened the menu and stabbed his finger at an entry. "Is the beef fresh?" He'd been to restaurants where they kept the meat hanging until it was green.

"Not as fresh as the catfish, sir. A swamper brings us a new catch each day. But I daresay the cook takes pride in her work and you'll find the beef as tasty as any, sir."

"No need for that," Fargo said.

"For what, sir?"

"All that sirring."

"There is a need, sir. If I don't, Mr. Hoffstedder will fire me. He's a stickler about his rules, and calling everybody sir is right at the top."

"Bring a pot of coffee," Fargo said, "and tell your cook to outdo herself."

"An entire pot, sir? Very well." The waiter bowed and walked off.

Fargo sat back, relaxing for the first time in days. As soon as he found General Canton and handed over the pouch, he'd head for the Rockies. Although, now that he thought about it, he should stick around a few days, to let the Ovaro rest.

The coffee came, piping hot and black, and after a couple of cups, Fargo felt the vinegar return to his veins. He was eagerly awaiting his steak when boots tramped and in walked Hoffstedder with a man wearing a badge.

The sheriff was short and lean and looked downright mean. He hadn't shaved in days and his clothes were badly rumpled. He wore a Remington high on his hip and a belt knife, besides. He also wore a constant scowl.

Hoffstedder pointed at Fargo and the sheriff marched up to Fargo's table and planted himself and announced, "I'm Sheriff Ashley."

"Good for you," Fargo said.

"That's not how you should talk to me. I'm not a man you want to cross."

"Makes two of us," Fargo said.

"So that's how it is," Ashley said. "I've only just met you but I can't say much for your attitude."

"Same here."

The lawman's scowl deepened. "How about if I cut this short and arrest you?"

4

Skye Fargo placed his right hand on the edge of the table above his holster. "If I'd broken a law I might let you. Since I didn't, you won't."

Sheriff Ashley stiffened. "You picked the wrong day to brace me," he said, and his own hand started to move along his belt toward his six-shooter.

"Gentlemen, please!" Hoffstedder said, stepping between them. "You're not roosters, for God's sake. This isn't a pecking contest." He shook a finger at Ashley. "Your job is to find the Night Terror, not intimidate my guests."

To Fargo's surprise, Ashley let his hand drop to his side.

"You're right. I'm letting it get to me. I've been at it so long, I'm not thinking straight."

"It would help if you got some sleep," Hoffstedder said. "When was the last time you had a good night's rest?"

"Sleep?" Ashley said. "What's that?"

Fargo pushed an empty chair out with his boot. "Why don't you join me, Sheriff? I have plenty of coffee and you look like a man who could use some."

Ashley hesitated, then sank down and tilted his hat back on his head. "This Night Terror has run me ragged."

"If that's all he's done, count your blessings," Fargo said. "He damn near killed me."

Both the sheriff and Hoffstedder said "What?" at the same time.

Fargo told them about his run-in with the apparition in the rain and how he found the head.

"Good God, man," Hoffstedder said. "You're lucky to be alive."

"What I want to know," Sheriff Ashley said, "is why the Terror didn't take your head?"

"Perhaps the thing is fussy," Hoffstedder said.

"That's just stupid," Ashley replied.

"Or maybe it wanted him to be able to report finding Jerrod Wilkes' head," Hoffstedder said, unflustered. "It always seems to want the heads to be found."

"No 'seems' about it," Ashley said.

"Whoever this killer is," Fargo interjected, "I owe him."

"Or whatever," Hoffstedder amended.

Sheriff Ashley swore. "Don't start with that again. It's a man. Not some spook or some monster."

"You're forgetting the tracks," Hoffstedder said. "You heard Mr. Fargo, here. He told us the tracks he saw had claws."

"I can't explain that," Ashley said, "yet."

"No offense, but you can't explain anything about this whole terrible business."

"It's not as if I'm not trying," the lawman said.

Hoffstedder glanced out the front window and reacted as if he'd been jabbed with a knife. "My word. Look at all those gawkers. I'd better go close the stable until you're ready to dispose of the head." He hurried away.

Ashley caught the waiter's attention and asked for a cup. He didn't speak again until he had filled it and taken several long swallows. "I'm grateful."

"Is it true the killing has been going on for two months?" Fargo said.

The sheriff nodded. "Seven good people murdered, and I'm no closer to catching the culprit than I was after the first."

Fargo would have thought it should be easy. "How many men around here are as big as the one I saw?"

"That's just it," Ashley said. "No one is."

"There has to be someone."

"I figured the same," Ashley said, "when I found the first tracks. I've asked everyone in Haven, all the folks living in the woods and the swamps, but no one has seen hide nor hair of a man as big as a bear."

"Well, damn."

"I've tried dogs but they only go as far as the swamp and lose the scent in the water."

"So the part about the Terror coming out of the swamp is genuine?"

"That's about the only part that is. The rest of it, that the thing is a haunt or a beast no one has ever seen before, has to be pure nonsense."

"Has to be," Fargo agreed, and noticed that the sheriff didn't seem so sure. "But . . . ?"

"But if it's a man, if it's flesh and blood, it's like no man I ever ran across," Ashley said quietly. "It comes and goes with hardly

13

anyone seeing it. The few times someone had caught a glimpse, it vanished in front of their eyes. And once, when I put dogs on it after finding a head, we chased it over ten miles at a pace that wore out the dogs but it was still going strong."

"It?" Fargo said.

"Force of habit," Ashley said. "Most everyone hereabouts calls the Night Terror 'it' and I find myself doing the same."

"Sooner or later he'll make a mistake and you'll have him."

"I hope to God you're right." Ashley coughed and looked out the window at the collection of curious souls. "Damn." He drained his cup and stood. "I'd like to talk to you again sometime but right now I'd better go help Hoffstedder disperse the crowd and see to that head."

"I'll be here a couple of days," Fargo mentioned. "If there's anything else you need to ask about."

"I'll keep it in mind."

The people out the window were growing animated. Two men raised their voices and were arguing. One poked the other and a fight was on the verge of breaking out when Sheriff Ashley waded in. He pushed the two men apart and barked commands and the rest began to move away.

Fargo told himself it was none of his business. He was there to deliver the dispatch pouch and that was all.

His food arrived. The steak was an inch and a half thick with a lot of fat. Fargo's mouth watered. He loved the soft, pulpy savor that melted in a man's mouth. Cutting a piece off, he chewed with relish. A heaping pile of potatoes smeared with butter and a generous helping of green beans made up the rest of the meal. He sprinkled salt over everything and ate ravenously.

Some folks didn't care much about food but he took his seriously. And food didn't get any better than fat, butter, and salt.

When he had eaten every morsel and dabbed his plate clean with the last of the bread, he sat back and patted his belly and came close to groaning with contentment.

"Would you care for dessert, sir?"

Fargo had been so invested in his meal, he hadn't sensed the waiter come up. To some it wouldn't matter but to him it was a lapse. "What do you have?"

"Apple pie or pudding. The pie was baked this morning and there's only one slice left so I would advise you to—"

Fargo looked up to see why the waiter had stopped. He'd heard the front door open but didn't think much of it until he saw that the waiter had blanched as if he'd seen the Night Terror.

Three men had entered. To say they were scruffy was an understatement. Their floppy hats and homespun clothes had seen better days. Their boots had holes. They were armed to the teeth, with rifles and pistols and knives and one had a hatchet, too.

They were gazing about as if dazzled by the elegance. Then the tallest spotted Fargo and poked the others and said something.

"Oh Lord," the waiter breathed.

"Who are they?" Fargo asked.

"Trouble. Awful trouble. I'd better go fetch Mr. Hoffstedder or, better yet, the sheriff."

The waiter made for the hall only to have his way barred by the three men, the youngest of whom grabbed him by the arm and hauled him with them as they approached Fargo's table.

"Where do think you're goin'?" said the one who had hold. "It's best you stick around."

"You don't want to cause trouble, Wayland Wilkes," the waiter said. "Mr. Hoffstedder wouldn't like it."

"As if I care what that hog likes," Wayland said, and imitated the squeal of the animal in question.

The other two laughed.

"The sheriff is right outside," the waiter said.

"We saw him," said the tall one.

"He don't scare us none," declared the third.

By then they were at the table. Wayland gave the waiter a push and leaned on the edge. "Introduce us."

The waiter looked as if he wanted to wilt into the floor. "These here are Wayland, Hosiah, and Abimelech Wilkes."

"We're brothers," Wayland said, as if it weren't obvious.

"Abimelech?" Fargo said.

The third brother bristled. "Don't you dare poke fun."

Wayland had a cleft chin and a comma of hair over his forehead. Hosiah was the tall one, all bone and sinew, with a beak of a nose an eagle would envy. As for Abimelech, he had no notable traits whatsoever.

"What can I do for you gents?" Fargo said.

"Ain't you polite?" Wayland responded.

"You'll sit there until we say you can get up," Hosiah said.

Abimelech nodded. "Or we'll pound you into the floor."

5

Fargo never liked being threatened. When he didn't reply right away, Abimelech leaned on the table with one hand and took hold of his buckskin shirt with the other.

"Cat got your tongue, mister? The least you can do is say somethin' or the poundin' will commence right quick."

"You've got that right, boy," Fargo said.

"I do?"

Too quick for the eye to follow, Fargo smashed his fist down on Abimelech's hand.

Abimelech howled and jerked his arm back and clasped his hurt hand to his chest. "He done hit me!"

"Consarn him anyhow," Wayland said.

"Are you two just goin' to stand there?" Abimelech cried.

"The mangy varmint," Hosiah snarled, and came around the table, hiking his rifle to bash the stock over Fargo's head.

Heaving up out of his chair, Fargo rammed his fist into Hosiah's gut while simultaneously grabbing the rifle and wrenching it loose. Hosiah staggered from the blow, and Fargo swung the rifle like a club. At the solid *thwack*, Hosiah dropped.

Wayland swore and lunged, swinging his own rifle. Fargo blocked and shoved, knocking Wayland back.

Abimelech was still holding his hand to his chest.

"Help me, damn it," Wayland hollered, and let go of his rifle to unlimber his hatchet.

Fargo had seldom used a hatchet but he'd used tomahawks on occasion. In the hands of an expert, they were a deadly weapon.

Wayland Wilkes came in fast but wary. He swung overhand. He swung underhand. He cleaved the hatchet from side to side.

Fargo countered with the rifle. He didn't care that the barrel was scraped or the stock was nicked. It wasn't his. Sidestepping when Wayland tried to take his leg off at the knee, he smashed the rifle into Wayland's face. Wayland screeched like a stuck cat and leaped out of reach, his nose streaming scarlet.

"Now, Abimelech! Now!"

Fargo had almost forgotten about the third brother. Abimelech had grabbed the steak knife off the table.

Pivoting, Fargo avoided a thrust at his back.

"You don't hurt us and get away with it!" Abimelech shouted.

Fargo let him rush in close. He flicked his boot, catching Abimelech on the knee. Cursing, Abimelech tried to skip back again but Fargo rammed the muzzle into his belly, and when Abimelech doubled over, swept the stock up and around.

That left Wayland, whose mouth and chin were covered with blood and who looked mad enough to tear into Fargo with his teeth. "These are your last moments. Do you hear me?"

"Prove it," Fargo taunted.

Wayland attacked in a frenzy. In his fury he didn't think to protect himself.

Fargo slammed the stock against Wayland's temple.

In the sudden silence, the waiter let out a long breath. "My word. You beat all three."

"They weren't much," Fargo said. Not compared to the Apaches. Or the Sioux. Or the Comanches. Or the . . .

"I'm afraid you've made mortal enemies," the waiter said. "They and their kin are good haters."

"Everyone should be good at something," Fargo said, and let the squirrel rifle fall to the floor.

"You're not taking this seriously enough," the waiter said. "Their whole clan will be out to get you."

"I'm trembling in my boots." Fargo sat back down and refilled his coffee cup.

Into the room rushed Sheriff Ashley. "Someone hollered there was a fight in here." He examined each of the unconscious men while more people came in from outside and fingers were pointed at Fargo and whispering broke out.

"They'll live," Ashley announced as he finished with Abimelech. "What was this about?" He directed the question at the waiter.

"They made threats against the gentleman in buckskins," the waiter said. "He didn't take kindly to it."

"I see." Ashley stepped to the table. "All three at once? You're a terror yourself, I reckon."

"They were more bark than bite," Fargo said.

The sheriff sighed. "I should have expected something like this to happen as soon as I heard the head belonged to a Wilkes. When one of their own is hurt or killed, they go to war."

"Makes you wonder who would kill Jerrod Wilkes, knowing that."

"It would give most anyone pause," Ashley agreed. "But then again, I half think the killer is a madman."

"Because he rips off heads?"

"Because there's no rhyme or reason to the attacks," Ashley said. "The Wilkes clan is dirt poor. The first victim came from a well-to-do family. None of the others have anything to do with one another." He frowned. "I suspect the killer picks whoever comes along when he's in a killing mood."

"He had a chance to kill me and didn't."

"I've been asking myself why ever since you told me. The only answer I can come up with puts things in a light I'd rather it didn't."

"Which is?"

"The only difference between you and all those the Night Terror has murdered," Sheriff Ashley said, "is that you're not from around these parts. You're not a local."

"That's something."

"It makes for more questions. Why only locals? What do they have in common that I'm missing? Why all these attacks now and not a year ago or five years ago? You can see why my head spins trying to make sense of it all, can't you?"

"I don't envy you," Fargo said.

Ashley turned, then paused. "About those buckskins of yours. What is it you do for a living?"

Fargo saw no reason to lie. Besides, he couldn't very well claim to be a clerk or a cowboy. "Mostly I work as a scout."

"I hear tell that scouts are good trackers."

"Some are."

"Any chance I can ask you for help if the Night Terror strikes again while you're here?"

Fargo shrugged. "I owe him for the conk on my noggin. But I'm only staying a couple of days."

"Too bad." Sheriff Ashley wearily rubbed his chin as he gazed out the window toward the stable. "Between you and me, I have a feeling the Night Terror isn't done with his spree. I worry there will be a heap more deaths before this is done unless I can catch him. And I'm at my wit's end."

"I wish you luck," Fargo said.

The sheriff's expression was grim. "I'll sure as hell need it."

6

Fargo had never met General Canton. He'd been told that the general wouldn't be in uniform, that Canton was posing as a civilian in order not to attract the interest of other parties who might want the information in the dispatch pouch.

Fargo's orders were to check in and wait, and Canton would make himself known. That's what he did. He registered and settled into a comfortable room on the second floor.

Stripping to the waist, he filled a china basin with water from a pitcher and washed the dust of the trail from his face and hair. He put on his spare shirt, slung the pouch across his chest as before, strapped his Colt around his waist, and ambled downstairs.

He figured that Canton must know he was there. Word of the severed head and the fight in the dining room had surely become common knowledge. He reckoned that if he walked around a while, the general would make himself known.

The grounds were a wonderment. Roses and lilacs and other flowers thrived. There were large stepping-stones for walkways. Guests promenaded about, enjoying the colors and the fragrances.

Fargo was admiring some of the reddest roses he'd ever seen when a light voice behind him gave a cattish trill.

"Oh my. What do we have here?"

"I do believe we've struck gold."

Fargo turned.

The pair was dazzling: lustrous hair, exquisitely coiffed, framed angelic faces with deviltry in their eyes. Their dresses rivaled the flowers for beauty. One had golden hair and the other's was a rich chestnut. They were about the same height and as shapely as two hourglasses.

"Fetch a parson, quick," Fargo said.

They looked quizzically at each other and then at him and the golden vision said, "Why a parson, of all things?"

"Because I must have died and gone to heaven and not known it until I saw you," Fargo bantered.

They laughed.

"Listen to you!" the blonde said.

"Clever *and* handsome as can be," said the chestnut-haired beauty. "You are a find, indeed. Who might you be?"

Fargo introduced himself.

"I'm Belinda and this is my best friend, Adelade," the blonde said. "We come to Havenpeak once a year to get away from city life for a spell."

"We're from New Orleans," Adelade mentioned.

"We do so love the gardens," Belinda said, gesturing at the red roses. "And the food and the service are superb."

"How about you?" Adelade asked. "Why are you here?"

"Passing through," was all Fargo was willing to say.

"Is this your first visit?" Belinda asked. "I bet it is. I'd remember if we'd ever set eyes on you before."

"Would we ever," Adelade said.

Fargo smiled. He liked that they were open about it. "I'll be here a couple of nights."

"Do tell," Belinda said, and she and her best friend giggled. "We have another week, ourselves."

"You're not worried about the Night Terror?"

"That silly monster?" Adelade said. "Why should we be? It only kills men."

"Fiddlesticks, I say," Belinda declared. "Why would it harm sweet little us? It hasn't ever hurt a guest, that we know of."

"Enough about that awful monster," Adelade said. "We're here to have fun and you look to me to be as fun as can be."

"Doesn't he, though?" Belinda said.

Fargo chuckled lustily. "Ladies, my stay here has become a whole lot more interesting."

"We should hope so," Adelade said.

Belinda grinned and nodded at Adelade and each of them took an arm. They walked with him between them, sashaying deeper into the gardens, their hips brushing his with every step.

"What would you like to do this evening?" Belinda asked.

"We're claiming you for our own," Adelade said.

"We insist you have fun," Belinda said.

"What do you like to do, anyhow?" Adelade said.

Fargo looked at one and then the other up and down, roving his hungry gaze from their red lips to their rounded bosoms to the outline of their thighs against their dresses as they walked. "Guess."

"My, oh my," Belinda said playfully. "I was right about striking gold."

They walked on, the ladies chattering merrily about life in New Orleans. The lilt of their accents, the grace of their movements, their refined humor—they were true Southern belles, "ladies" in every sense.

They were not at all like the doves Fargo usually dallied with, not that the doves weren't ladies too. They made him grin and laugh and forget about everything except them, which was the whole point to their flirtatious teasing. He took such delight in their company that he forgot all about his special assignment for the army until Adelade leaned toward him and whispered in his ear.

"Don't look now, handsome, but I do believe someone is following us."

Fargo checked an impulse to look over his shoulder. "Where?"

It was Belinda who answered. "Behind us a ways. Gentleman with a trimmed beard and a cane, in dark clothes. He stops when we stop and goes on when we do. And he keeps looking at us when he thinks we won't notice."

"That's the one," Adelade said.

They came to some magnolias. Fargo slid his arms free, plucked a flower with each hand, and gave one to Belinda and Adelade. As he did, he peered from under his hat brim at a middling-sized man dressed in the same elegant manner as Hoffstedder. Only on him the clothes fit better. The man was staring at them but quickly looked away.

"Well, now," Fargo said.

"Are we right?" Adelade whispered.

"What will you do?" Belinda asked.

"Let's keep walking," Fargo said, and clasping their elbows, he steered them around the magnolias and over to a fountain. Large goldfish swam lazily in the pool. Stone benches had been provided, and he ushered the ladies to the nearest.

"Have a seat."

"What are you fixing to do?" Belinda asked.

"No matter what happens, stay put."

"But you haven't told us what you'll be doing," Adelade said.

"Pretending I'm a piece of cheese." Fargo moved around the fountain and over to a path between high hedges. A quick glance showed that the man in the dark coat was ignoring Belinda and Adelade and following him.

Fargo moved along the path. At the first junction he ducked to one side and pressed his back to the hedge. His hand on his Colt, he waited, expecting to hear footfalls or the tap of the man's cane.

A wren chirped somewhere and in the distance a dog barked but no one came along the path.

Perplexed, Fargo straightened. He wondered if he was mistaken, that the man in the dark coat was just a guest out for a stroll. He stepped around the corner and stopped cold as the gleaming tip of a pointed blade was thrust at his throat.

The tip pricked Fargo's skin. He froze, knowing that he was as good as dead if he didn't.

"Any sudden moves," the man in the dark coat said, "and I'll skewer you."

"I believe you," Fargo said.

The man's trimmed beard was a reflection of the rest of his appearance. Even though he was in civilian garb, everything about him was spit and polish. He held his sword cane in a way that suggested he was well versed in its use. "Confirm for me that you're Skye Fargo. You fit the description but I can't take a chance that you're not."

"Confirm it how, General?" Fargo said. "All Colonel Hastings at Fort Laramie told me was to find you. My horse knows who I am but I doubt that helps much."

General Canton lowered his sword and with a flourish slid the blade into the cane. "A silly business, this skulking around like a pair of spies. But Washington wants to keep it secret."

"Keep what secret?"

The general looked about them. "Not here. Too many ears. Come with me." He moved along the hedge path, turned right, and continued until they were in the open. Ahead sat another stone bench that overlooked the settlement of Haven and the sprawl of swamp and forest that stretched to the horizon. "There will do. No one can come close without us seeing them."

Fargo followed him to the bench but didn't sit when the general did. He was more interested in the sleepy hamlet. Unless his eyes deceived him, there was a saloon down there.

"Now then," Canton said. "How much were you told?"

"To give you the pouch."

"That's all?" Canton swore. "Typical. The fate of the nation in the offing and they can't be bothered to make that clear."

Fargo tore his gaze from the saloon. Tapping the dispatch pouch, he said, "The fate of the nation? In here?"

General Canton placed both hands on the handle of his cane.

"In a very real sense, yes. You're aware, are you not, that a number of Southern states are on the verge of seceding, and that if they do, war will break out?"

"I know there's been a lot of talk."

"It's well beyond that stage, I'm afraid," Canton said. "The politicians have reached an impasse. Soon the United States government might find itself fighting its own citizens."

Fargo looked at the pouch. "This fits in how?"

"The War Department has been quietly taking steps to prepare. I stress quietly. The president doesn't want to provoke the other side any more than they already are. If they find out the army has been secretly making a tally of our military resources west of the Mississippi, they'll say that the president's peace efforts are a sham and he's really wanted war all along."

"Why not do it out in the open?"

General Canton frowned. "Yes, we could have had someone in the inspector general's office go from post to post and be above-board in all he did. But that would be just as bad, don't you think? Once the other side got wind of it, they'd accuse us of gearing for war. And we couldn't very well deny it."

"So you did it in secret."

"Now if they accuse us, we can deny it because they won't have any proof." General Canton paused. "Unless they were to get their hands on the report that's in your pouch. It's the only one in existence, a complete inventory of our troops and supplies and states of readiness on the Western frontier." He held out a hand. "I will relieve you of it."

Fargo was glad to be shed of the thing. He slid the strap over his head and off his shoulder. "One last question."

"You're entitled," Canton said.

"Why me?" Fargo asked. "Why not Colonel Harrington or some other officer? Hell, why not any sergeant or trooper?"

"Several reasons. The first is that even in civilian clothes, sometimes there's no mistaking a military bearing."

Fargo grunted. The general had a point. One look at him and Fargo had known.

"Reason number two is that we're not entirely sure who we can trust among our own ranks. Sad to say, but many of our officers and enlisted men harbor sympathies for the South. What if we unwittingly entrusted the report to one of them?"

"The last reason?"

"We needed someone dependable. Someone we could count on

to get through. You, Mr. Fargo, have earned that reputation. You also have a reputation for—shall I say, lewd behavior? Despite that, and despite your fondness for whiskey and cards, you're still regarded as one of the best scouts we have."

"Lewd?" Fargo said.

"As General Fairbanks put it to me, you have what he called 'female fever.'"

Fargo had met Fairbanks a few times. A good officer, fair and resolute. "That's what he thinks of me?"

"To be more exact, he said that if you so much as catch a whiff of a friendly skirt, you are halfway up it before the woman can blink."

Fargo laughed.

"And as I say, despite that, we decided that you were the man for the job." General Canton gestured. "The pouch, if you please."

Fargo gave it to him.

"You need not be offended by that female fever business," Canton said. "I daresay there isn't an officer of my acquaintance who doesn't envy your, um, record."

"I'll be damned," Fargo said.

Canton propped his cane against the stone bench and opened the pouch. He pulled out a sheath of papers bound in a leather cover. "Not much to it, is there? Yet it might be the key to our winning the war in the West."

"Why meet here, of all places?"

"I grew up in these parts. I have family here. I'd been to Havenpeak Inn before, so it wouldn't arouse suspicion if I came for a visit."

It still seemed to Fargo like a lot of bother to go to. "Now that you have it, what next?"

"I leave for Washington in the morning." General Canton stood and removed his hat and coat. Sliding the pouch strap over his head and left arm, he put his coat and hat back on and sat down. "There. No one will know I have it."

"All these shenanigans," Fargo said.

"They might seem pointless to you but I assure you they're not. In several days I will personally place this report on the president's desk, and you'll have done us an inestimable service."

"Happy to help." Fargo would be happier if he could pay a visit to that saloon in Haven. "If there's nothing else . . ."

"There is, in fact," Canton said. "What's this I hear about you tangling with the Night Terror?"

"Oh. That."

"Most people think the murders are random but I'm not so sure. I'd like to hear every detail."

Reluctantly, Fargo complied.

"Interesting," Canton said when he was done. "That this Night Terror didn't kill you is proof in my mind that he doesn't work for the other side." Rising, he turned toward the hedge and gave a start. "What do those three want? I wonder."

Fargo looked and felt a surge of anger.

Coming toward them were Wayland, Hosiah, and Abimelech Wilkes.

8

Fargo stepped around the stone bench and the general. "These are my nuisances to deal with."

"I know those men," Canton said. "I told you I was raised here."

The three Wilkeses advanced abreast with their rifles in their hands. They stopped when Fargo placed his hand on his Colt. "That's far enough."

"We've been lookin' for you, mister," Wayland said.

"We're not done with you," Hosiah said.

"Not by a long shot," Abimelech said. "We aim to hear about our cousin whether you like it or not."

General Canton cleared his throat. "Here now. What's this about? You're some of the Wilkes boys, as I recall."

"Do we know you?" Wayland said, then tilted his head. "Wait. You're the oldest of the Canton brood. The ones with rich kin in Virginia or someplace."

"That's right," Hosiah said. "Didn't we hear a long time ago that you went off to—what's it called? West Point?"

"I did, in fact," General Canton said.

"And there you stand in your fancy duds," Abimelech said. "You don't look or sound like one of us anymore."

"Experience changes a man, boys," the general said.

"If'n you say so," Wayland replied. "And it'd best change this Daniel Boone's mind about talkin' to us."

"Sure better," Hosiah echoed.

"Is that all you want to do? Talk?" General Canton asked.

"We want to hear about him findin' our cousin's head," Hosiah said. "No one does that to a Wilkes and gets away with it."

Abimelech nodded. "Whoever or whatever it was, we're goin' to make gator meat out of 'em."

"Where did you find it?" Wayland asked. "And did you see what was to blame?"

"*That's* all you wanted?" Fargo said. "Why didn't you say so before?"

"You never gave us no chance."

Fargo almost felt a twinge of regret. "You didn't act like all you wanted to do was talk."

"That's neither here nor there," Hosiah said. "All we're interested in is the party that done it, be it man or beast."

"An eye for an eye," Abimelech said.

"It's in the Bible," Wayland said.

"So what can you tell us?" Hosiah said.

Reluctantly, Fargo related it again. The Wilkeses listened intently. Wayland was the first to speak when he was done.

"Well, damn. It's the same as all the other attacks. You didn't get a good look at it and don't know nothin' exceptin' it's big and it's strong."

"How are we goin' to find it?" Abimelech said.

"I have a question," General Canton said. "Why do you suppose the Night Terror attacked your cousin? Is there anything he had in common with the other victims?"

"He was a local, like us. And male. That's about all the common there is," Hosiah said.

"Do you happen to know where he was when he was attacked?" Canton probed. "Was he at home? Off coon hunting? In town?"

"That's the only thing we do know," Wayland said. "We talked to his missus. She told us they were at supper and he got up to go use the outhouse and never came back."

"She never heard nothin', neither," Hosiah said. "He got up and went out and was gone so long, she got to wonderin' what was keepin' him and went for a look-see and found the outhouse door hangin' open but there was no sign of Jerrod anywhere."

"He'd done disappeared," Abimelech said.

"Interesting," General Canton said. "It sounds as if the Night Terror was waiting for him."

Wayland said, "Jerrod weren't nothin' but a fun-lovin' boy like us. He liked to hunt and drink and scratch hisself. What's there to kill him for over that?"

"Was your cousin political?" the general asked.

"Politi-what?" Abimelech said.

"The North–and–the South business," General Canton said. "Surely you've heard about it."

"Oh. That," Wayland said. "Us Wilkes ain't ever been rich enough to have slaves, so what do we care what that Yankee president thinks?"

"I must say," General Canton said. "These deaths mystify me."

"We didn't care none about them, either, until the Terror kilt our cousin," Wayland declared. To Fargo he said, "We won't bother you no more. And no hard feelin's about the fight. Truth is, it was the most fun we've had in months."

"Let's go," Hosiah said. "We're wastin' daylight and we've got us a Night Terror to find."

The three brothers turned and walked off.

"Remarkable," General Canton said. "You'd never imagine to look at them that they possess such fortitude."

Fargo was just glad they hadn't come to blows. "Is there anything else?"

"Between us?" the general said. "No. You've completed your mission and are free to do as you please. Your country and I thank you." He held out his hand.

Fargo shook.

"I doubt I'll run into you before I leave in the morning but if I do, it's best if we act as if we don't know each other. You understand why, of course?"

"Who are you again?" Fargo said.

General Canton laughed. "What will you do with yourself to pass the time?"

In his mind's eye, Fargo pictured the saloon filled with whiskey guzzlers and doves parading around and could practically hear the clink of bottles and glasses and the clatter of poker chips. "I'll think of something."

9

The saloon was called the Quicksand. Why anyone would name a saloon that was beyond Fargo, but it was a whiskey mill and that was all that counted. He pushed on the batwings and strolled in with a smile on his face and after taking only two steps he stopped and looked around and said, "What the hell?"

The place was deserted. The tables were bare, the chairs empty, the bar unoccupied except for an old man behind it, leaning on his elbow and dozing.

Striding over, Fargo smacked the counter.

The old man jumped and blinked and then showed his yellow teeth in a friendly grin. "What'll it be, stranger?"

"People," Fargo said.

"Eh?" The old man cupped a hand to his left ear. "You'll have to speak up, sonny. I don't hear so good no more. I could have sworn you just said you wanted people to drink."

"Where are the ladies?" Fargo said.

"You want to drink a female? How in tarnation would you do that? It's the silliest notion I've ever heard."

"Where are they?" Fargo said, and gestured at the empty saloon. "Why isn't anyone else here?"

"Oh. That." The old man chuckled. "Folks won't drift in here until along about sundown. I'm Skellion, by the way."

"Skellion?"

"On account of that's what I like to eat more than anything. I like the white ones more than the purple ones 'cause the whites are sweeter."

Fargo got a whiff of his breath. "Been eating some today, I take it."

"Breakfast and supper and in between," Skellion said. "Sometimes I smear them on me just so's I'll smell good."

"The bayou country," Fargo said.

"What about it?" Skellion said. "And we ain't strictly bayou folks, you know. We're sort of at the edge. I'd guess you'd call us bayou and hill country. Or since the hills are so puny, bayou and puny hill country."

Fargo stared.

"What?"

"You do sell whiskey?"

"We're a saloon, ain't we?" Skellion turned to a shelf laden with bottles. "Anyone ever tell you that you're a mite peculiar?"

"Bayou and puny hill country," Fargo said, and laughed.

"You just got that? Peculiar *and* slow." Skellion set a dusty bottle in front of Fargo and blew on it with his "skellion" breath. He opened it, produced a glass, and filled it to the brim. "Here you go."

"You can have that." Fargo took the bottle, tilted it to his lips, and chugged. In three gulps he downed a third of the bottle. Smacking his lips, he let out a contented sigh. "Right fine coffin varnish."

Skellion picked up the glass with delicate care, as if afraid to spill a drop. He sipped, and smiled his yellow smile, and said, "I take back what I said about you bein' peculiar. You're a true gent, and that's no lie."

"About the ladies . . ." Fargo said.

"We don't sell any to drink, no."

"Where could I find a friendly one?"

"Over to the church all the ladies are friendly. Except for those as walk around with their noses in the air. But we ain't got many of those, thank God." Skellion paused. "Mrs. Eberhouser just down the street, you go and knock on her door and she'll give you milk and cookies."

Fargo did more staring.

"What?"

"When I say friendly, I mean really friendly," Fargo said, and winked.

"What's friendlier than milk and cookies?"

"That's not the kind of friendly I mean," Fargo said, and winked a couple of times.

"Somethin' wrong with your eye? It keeps twitchin'."

"God," Fargo said, and treated himself to another swig.

"I take back what I said about takin' back what I said about you bein' peculiar," Skellion said.

Fargo came right out with it. "Does Haven have any ladies who do it for money?"

"It? What's it?"

"You know."

"Oh. You mean fornicatin' and such?"

"I could hit you."

"Hey now. No need to be mean. If'n all you wanted was a poke, why didn't you come right out and say so?"

"I'm saying it now."

"Sheriff Ashley ain't fond of tarts. He says they cause nothin' but trouble."

"Figures," Fargo said and sighed.

"We do have Sadie, though."

"Who?"

"She works here, nights. Sometimes she'll let a fella poke her if'n she takes a shine to him or needs drinkin' money."

"Where do I find her?"

"Probably at her place."

Fargo waited, and when the old man didn't go on, he asked, "Where would that be?"

"Where it's always been. You go left out the batwings and walk two blocks and there's a sign that says SADIE'S."

"She has a sign?"

"I just said she did, didn't I? You ask me, you hear worse than I do."

Fargo fished out his poke to pay for the bottle and idly asked, "Do you get a lot of customers after the sun goes down these days?"

"Why wouldn't I?"

"The Night Terror."

A hint of fear came into Skellion's eyes. "Why'd you have to bring that critter up? Gives me the jeebies just thinkin' of that thing rippin' heads off."

"So you don't think it's a man?"

"Hell, no. It's a swamp beast. Like those skunk apes, only worse."

Fargo was aware that in parts of the South, there was a widespread belief that a type of ferocious ape lived deep in the swamps. "You must hear a lot of talk."

"It's all anybody jabbers about these days," Skellion said. "They're scared, people are. And I can't blame 'em." He stopped and glanced at the batwings. "I saw it once, you know."

"The Night Terror?" Fargo said skeptically.

Skellion bobbed his chin and his Adam's apple bobbed, too. "It was late one night after I'd closed up and was takin' some trash out to the burn pile. I heard a sound and looked over and there it was, as huge as anything."

"Could it have been a bear?"

"Hell, no. My ears don't work so good but my eyes work fine. Besides, it was a full moon, and I saw it almost as plain as I see you. It was the Night Terror, standin' there sniffin'."

"Sniffing what?"

"The air, you lunkhead. It was off toward the church. I couldn't see its face but I saw how hairy it was, and how it was sort of hunched over, like, with its front paws almost scrapin' the ground." Skellion stopped and raised a sleeve to his perspiring brow.

"I about wet myself, I was so scared."

"What did it do?"

"I already told you. It sniffed. It must not have smelled me, though, or seen me, 'cause it went off into the dark and I came back in and lay in my bed and shivered until mornin'."

"You really think it's a swamp beast?"

Skellion lowered his voice to a whisper. "That's what I tell everybody. But between you and me, that's not what I think it is at all."

"What then?"

Skellion said in all earnestness, "The Night Terror is a demon out of hell."

10

There was a sign sure enough. It read SADIE's in pink letters.

Fargo went onto the porch and knocked. He'd brought his bottle of Monongahela and an extra, besides. Inside, shoes clunked on a hardwood floor. The door opened and a cloud of perfume tingled his nose. "You must be Sadie."

She was a surprise. Not much over twenty, she had hair the color of a carrot and a body most men would drool over. Her dress was pink, like her sign, as were the tips of the shoes that poked from under it. Her cheeks were pink, too, and her lips even more so. "I do declare," she said in a husky purr. "What have we here?"

"Skellion over at the saloon said you're the friendliest gal in town."

"That old coot," Sadie said, and laughed.

"I had to practically wrestle it out of him," Fargo mentioned.

"He fooled you. I pay him ten cents to send men my way. If you hadn't said a word, he'd have brought me up on his own."

"That crafty buzzard," Fargo said.

"That's Skellion, all right." Sadie moved aside and motioned. "Why don't you come in and make yourself comfortable?"

The house had a lilac scent and was spotlessly clean. Her tasteful parlor included a settee with cushions. Pink, of course. She sat and patted a cushion to indicate he should take a seat.

"For you," Fargo said, offering her the extra bottle. "Skellion said you're fond of whiskey."

"Fond is putting it mildly," Sadie said, accepting it. "I thank you for your kindness. Now what can I do for you?"

Fargo looked at her bosom. "Guess."

"Did Skellion happen to mention that I only do it if I take a powerful shine to the fella?"

"How long does that take?"

Sadie laughed. "In a rush, are you?"

"I've gone without for more than ten days," Fargo said.

"That long, huh?" Sadie placed her warm hand on his knee. "You men are always in a rush. A gal likes to take her time, get acquainted first."

"Oh, hell."

Sadie laughed louder. "If men were more patient, us women would be a lot more willing."

"I've never had any complaints," Fargo said. "What else do you need to know to take that shine to me?"

"Listen to you." Sadie settled back. "Since I'm the only filly in town, you'll have to play by my rules."

"I saw other ladies," Fargo said.

"But not as will lift their skirts for men they hardly know. There are laws against that."

"How come the sheriff lets you?" Fargo wondered.

"Sheriff Ashley believes that men will always be men, and that they need what he calls an outlet for their needs."

"You're the outlet?"

"I'm not the parson."

"So do you know me enough now?" Fargo asked.

Sadie cackled. "Your patience is pitiful. I usually take half an hour or more to warm up to a gentleman."

"We could strip bare and rub our bodies together," Fargo proposed. "That would warm us up quicker."

It wasn't to be. Sadie made small talk about Haven and growing up in that neck of the woods and how much she loved lilacs and butterflies and finches and cookies.

"I could go on and on," she finally concluded, "but I fear you'd fall asleep."

"I'm bright-eyed and bushy-tailed," Fargo lied.

"Tell me a little about yourself. You got a gal anywhere?"

"No."

"What do you like to do?"

"Drink, gamble, and screw."

Sadie snorted. "We're back to that again."

"We never left it."

Sadie stood and smoothed her dress. "I reckon it's time we got to it, then. Let me hang my sign out and we can commence."

"There's another sign?"

Nodding as she moved toward the hall, Sadie said, "I got the idea from the sawbones. He has a sign he hangs in his window when he's out that says THE DOCTOR ISN'T IN RIGHT NOW. So I had a sign made that says the same, only with my name. So I'm not disturbed in the middle of a poke."

Fargo drummed his fingers on the settee until she returned and beckoned. Clasping his arm, she led him to a flight of stairs and up

35

to one of several bedrooms. Everything was pink, from the curtains to the quilt to the doily on a bed table. She lit a candle even though the sun wouldn't set for hours.

"I like the scent," Sadie said when he asked why. "This one here smells like vanilla."

"I'd rather smell you."

"What a sweet thing to say." Sadie pried at the top button on the front of her dress. "I can't say the same about a lot of the men who pay me a visit. Some haven't bathed in a month of Sundays, if ever. Thank God for scented candles..They spare my nose a lot of misery."

Fargo sat on the edge of the bed to remove his spurs and boots. Now that they were finally getting down to it, he found himself wanting to take his time. "What can you tell me about the Night Terror?"

Sadie froze with a button half undone. "Why on earth would you bring that up? I'm sick to death of hearing about the killings. It's all anyone is talking about."

"Skellion told me he thinks it's a demon."

"He drinks too much of his own liquor," Sadie said, continuing to pry at buttons. "Whatever or whoever the Night Terror is, it's no laughing matter."

"Do you hear me laughing?"

"One of those it killed was a friend of mine," Sadie revealed. "A good customer by the name of Mac. Short for McGregor. He had a small farm out west of here. They found his body in his cabin and his head in his barn."

"Any idea why the Night Terror killed him?"

"No. Although he was acting peculiar the last time I saw him. As if he was afraid of something." Sadie closed her eyes, then opened them again. "Enough about that awful brute. You'll spoil my mood if you keep it up. I pray to God the sheriff catches it soon and puts an end to its horrible spree."

The last thing Fargo wanted was for her to change her mind. Moving closer, he pressed flush to her body while cupping her bottom. "Consider him forgotten."

"Prove it."

Her lips were hot and soft and luscious. He let the kiss linger as she squirmed and cooed and kneaded his shoulders.

"Not bad," Sadie said when they broke for breath.

"There's a lot more where that came from." Kneading her backside, Fargo nipped her ear and licked her neck. He cupped a breast and squeezed and she rose onto her toes as if trying to take wing.

"Do that again," she husked.

Fargo did, and presently they were on the bed, as bare as the day they were born. He took a few moments to admire the sweep of her taut breasts with their nipples erect like tacks. Inhaling one, he licked while his hands were busy lower down. With one he caressed the velvet smoothness of her inner thighs. With the other he ran a finger along her moist slit and made her shiver.

After that, they were lost in each other, giving full release to their carnal cravings. Sadie liked to do everything and was as tireless as he was.

When, eventually, they nearly broke the bed with their mutual explosion, Fargo fell back, spent and tired and slick with sweat. "Nice," he heard her say as she smiled dreamily and drifted off.

Fargo let himself do the same. He figured to nap a little and be at the saloon by sunset but when he opened his eyes the shade over the window was gray with twilight.

Careful not to wake Sadie, Fargo dressed and strapped on his Colt. He left a double eagle on the night table.

Downstairs, the house was growing dark. He remembered his bottle of Monongahela and got it from the parlor on his way out.

The sun was gone, the air muggy, the heat of the day not yet dissipated by the cool of encroaching night. He stood on the porch and yawned and stretched, then shook himself to get his blood flowing.

At the same instant, across the street, a gun boomed.

11

The act of tossing his head to clear it saved his life. The slug that was intended to core his brain missed his head by a whisker and struck the front doorjamb behind him. Instinctively, Fargo crouched and drew his Colt.

The gun boomed a second time, a rifle by the sound of it, and slivers went flying from the porch rail.

Fargo spied the muzzle flash. The shooter was in dark shadow between two houses. Fanning the Colt twice, he was off the porch in a bound, weaving as he charged to the street. He was ready for the rifle to fire again but it didn't.

Reaching the same shadows, he glimpsed someone running around the rear of the house on the left and gave chase.

Fargo had no idea who was trying to kill him. The Wilkes brothers had wanted only information and he had no enemies in Haven that he knew of. He raced around the corner and spied the shooter running flat out, a slender figure on the spare side wearing what looked to be a woolen cap, of all things.

The figure melted into the darkness.

Fargo poured on speed and ran over fifty yards before he stopped in frustration. The shooter had vanished. He roved from yard to yard but the would-be assassin was gone.

Venting an oath, Fargo reloaded. He was surprised that no one had come to investigate the shots, but then again, this was back-woods country where guns were as common as fleas and the locals were used to gunshots all hours of the day and night.

Twirling the Colt into his holster, Fargo bent his boots to the Ovaro. He'd changed his mind about the saloon. The attempt on his life might be tied to the pouch he'd delivered, although why anyone would want to kill him when he no longer had it was beyond him.

Still, General Canton needed to be warned.

The dirt road up the hill meandered like a snake.

Night had fallen and the frogs in the swamp were making the air thrum. Once, in the distance, a gator bellowed, and closer, in the woods, a bobcat screeched.

It wasn't the Rockies or the prairie but Fargo felt the same thrill of being in the wilds. In a way, the wild places were as intoxicating as the whiskey he was so fond of. They got into a man's blood and filled him with a feeling that was hard to describe, of being keenly alive and not just going through the motions that most town and city dwellers did.

A safe life was a dull life and Fargo hated dull more than he hated just about anything.

Havenpeak Inn loomed at the crest, its many windows ablaze. The gardens, too, were speckled with the glow of lanterns that hung from posts.

Fargo rode to the stable and left the Ovaro with Eli, telling him not to strip the saddle. He went into the inn and asked at the desk if the clerk happened to know Canton's whereabouts. He was taken aback when the clerk consulted the register and informed him that no one by that name was staying there.

Fargo thanked him and walked off. He realized the general must be traveling under an assumed name to throw off "the other side," and he hadn't thought to ask what it was.

Games of deceit weren't to Fargo's liking. At least with an Apache or a Comanche, he knew who his enemies were. Here it could be anyone.

The general hadn't told him what room he was in, either, so Fargo had no choice but to stroll about the inn and then the grounds in the hope of spotting him. He wasted a lot of valuable drinking time.

He went through the gardens twice and decided Canton must have gone to bed in order to get an early start in the morning. Figuring he might as well head back down to Haven, he walked around to the front of the inn, and there, on the portico, was the man himself, smoking a cigar.

"Here you are."

Canton smiled and flicked ash from his cigar. "I like a smoke right before I turn in. It helps relax me."

"This one could get you shot."

"I've seen no evidence of the opposition," Canton said. He patted his jacket where it bulged from the dispatch pouch. "And the secret report is safe."

"If no one is after it," Fargo said, "maybe you can explain who'd want to put a window in my skull?"

"How's that again?"

Fargo told him about the try on his life.

"Well, now. This is disturbing." Canton flicked his cigar, his brow furrowed in thought. "Someone must suspect you of still having the pouch. Or . . ." He stopped and chewed his bottom lip.

"What?" Fargo prompted.

"Or they know you've passed the packet to me and wanted you out of the way so you couldn't interfere when they try to take it from me."

To Fargo that seemed far-fetched and he said so.

"In affairs like this," General Canton said, "nothing is ever as it seems." He straightened. "In any event, I doubt the attempt on your life was random. It proves the other side is here, and it behooves me to act accordingly. Instead of leaving at dawn, as I'd intended, I'll depart within the hour."

"At night?"

"They won't expect it. If they've been watching me, they might have heard me tell the desk clerk that I'll be settling my bill in the morning." Canton nodded to himself. "Yes, by God. By leaving now, I'll throw them off the scent." He wheeled and strode inside.

Fargo went along. He had a feeling the general was making a mistake and offered, "I'll ride with you a spell to be sure it's safe."

"That's not necessary but I thank you."

The general was already packed except for his shaving kit and toiletries. He threw them into a small travel bag and together they descended to the desk.

Fargo studied every face but no one showed any interest.

The clerk expressed surprise that "Mr. Smith" was leaving at such an unusual hour. Canton told him that he needed to be in Kansas City before the week was out.

"If the other side questions him," the general remarked as he and Fargo approached the stable, "they'll take the wrong road. I'm actually heading south to New Orleans and from there to Washington."

After Eli saddled the general's mount, Canton hooked his travel bag over the saddle horn and they were under way.

Haven lay quiet under the sparkling stars. That late at night, only the saloon was open. Several horses were at the hitch rail but it looked to be as dead as the cemetery.

Fargo's skin prickled as they passed down the main street. The shooter might still be there, awaiting another chance. But they made it to the end of the sleepy hamlet without incident.

Ahead stretched countless miles of woodland and swamp. Soon the road narrowed until it was barely wide enough for a wagon.

From all sides rose the squeals and cries and shrieks of nature in the raw. Night brought the gators out in force, as well as a legion of four-legged meat-eaters, from painters to bears.

"Are you sure about this?" Fargo asked after a black bear grunted close to the road.

"I'm not a child, Mr. Fargo," General Canton said. "I'm not afraid of the dark. Surely you're not, either."

No, Fargo wasn't. But there was a thing called common sense, and daring the dangers of the bayou country in the dead of night didn't strike him as smart.

"You keep forgetting I was raised here," General Canton reminded him. "To me, this is home. I roamed these swamps as a boy. I played in these woods. They bring back many fond memories."

"I bet most of them were in the daylight."

Canton laughed. "Even so, a grown man must put away the fears of childhood. So long as I stick to the road I'll be fine."

Fargo didn't share his confidence. A road meant nothing to a snake or a panther—or a shooter.

"When I retire I plan to come back to Haven and live out my days hunting and fishing and doing other things I enjoyed in my youth. Have you ever gone coon hunting? Or waded a creek after crawdads?"

The Ovaro's ears suddenly pricked. Fargo thought he heard it, too; the faint clomp of a hoof—behind them. Shifting in the saddle, he probed the darkness but saw no one.

"What is it?" General Canton asked.

"I'm not sure."

"For a scout you're terribly jumpy. You need to relax. No one can get at us without us hearing them."

Fargo could, and if he could, so could others.

"I feel safer out here than I did at the inn," Canton was saying. "I never knew but someone might stick a knife in my back."

"They still might," Fargo said.

"I tell you I know these swamps. Trust me when I say that nothing out here can surprise me."

No sooner were the words out of the general's mouth than the night was shattered by an inhuman roar.

12

They both drew rein, and the general blurted, "My word. What in the world was that?"

Fargo had heard that roar before. The memory brought a twinge of pain to his head, and he involuntarily broke out in a sweat. "The Night Terror."

"It must have been a bear. A bear and nothing more. Unless . . ."

"Unless what?" Fargo said when the general didn't go on.

Canton appeared paler and was nervously rubbing his chin. "I just remembered what my grandmother told me about the Petries."

"The who?"

"You did say the thing that attacked you moved like a man and was huge, did you not?"

"Like a man and like an animal, too," Fargo said.

"My God," General Canton said. "Can it be? I'd nearly forgotten, it's been so long since . . ."

Again Fargo had to prod him. "Since what?"

"Nothing," Canton said, shaking his head. "I must be mistaken. It can't be, not after all this time." He clucked to his zebra dun.

Fargo wasn't about to let it drop. "Who are the Petries?"

"The wealthiest family in these parts," General Canton answered. "Or they were, until about ten years ago. There's irony for you."

Another cry rent the wilds, this one more a wail than a roar. It keened on the wind, sorrow given sound, fearsome and haunting at the same time.

"Good Lord," the general exclaimed. He shook his head and muttered and lapsed into silence.

Twice Fargo tried to get him to talk about it and each time Canton replied, "I must be mistaken."

Fargo had intended to accompany Canton a couple of miles and then turn back. With the Night Terror abroad, he decided to stick with him until daybreak, if not longer.

Midnight came and went. The terrain became more swamp than woodland, and often brackish water lapped at the road's edge.

The chorus of frogs and gators would rise to a crescendo and then, in the bat of an eye, the swamp would become totally quiet, as if an unseen presence had frightened every living thing into silence.

Yet another reason Fargo hated swamps. He'd been to a few in his travels, down in Louisiana and Texas and elsewhere. Each and every time he'd been lucky to get out alive. They were treacherous, unpredictable, and deadly, and as alien as the moon.

Give him the mountains and the plains. Give him solid earth under his feet, not mud and bogs and quicksand. Give him the wide open spaces, not tangles of rank vegetation that clung and clawed like the animals themselves. And don't get him started on those animals. When a buffalo or a grizzly came at him, he could nearly always see it coming. Not alligators. They rose out of the depths and were on a man before the man realized they were there. To say nothing of cottonmouths and other snakes.

To his way of thinking, a swamp was the closest thing to hell on earth. Even a desert was better. In a desert you might die of thirst. A swamp had a thousand ways to kill you.

"Do you hear that?" General Canton asked.

Fargo gave a start. He'd been so deep in thought, he hadn't caught the faint sound of crackling and snapping, as of something huge crashing through the heavy growth, not caring who or what knew it was there.

"A bear, you think?"

Fargo doubted it. Bears often made noise but not that much. "Could be," was all the further he'd commit himself.

The sounds faded and for all of a minute the swamp was still. Then bedlam erupted.

"I'm glad you're along," General Canton said. "I don't mind admitting that I find all this unnerving."

"Who wouldn't?"

"I shouldn't, though," Canton said. "I'm a soldier. Conquering fear is my stock-in-trade."

Fargo remembered the hoof fall he'd heard earlier and looked over his shoulder. Near as he could tell, no one was back there.

"You should come with me to New Orleans," the general unexpectedly remarked. "The night life will be to your liking."

Fargo had been there, and it was. Next to Denver, it had more ladies of the night than just about anywhere. The liquor flowed freely and there were card games to sit in on all hours of the day and night.

A mosquito buzzed near his ear and Fargo swatted at it.

The road was taking them ever deeper into the swamp. Not so much as a single campfire lit the blackness. It was as if the primeval had swallowed them whole and they were moving through a nightmare realm of creatures running amok.

"I can't believe I used to go out into the swamp at night when I was little all by myself," General Canton reminisced. "I must have been braver back then." He laughed without mirth.

Fargo was straining to hear hoofbeats. If someone was trailing them, sooner or later they'd give it away.

The general suddenly drew rein. "There it is again. What in the world is it?"

The crackling and snapping was back, only louder. Something was coming toward them, or toward the road, which amounted to the same thing. As it had done before, the creature gave voice to a wail that prickled the short hairs at the nape of Fargo's neck.

"It almost sounds human," General Canton breathed.

"Almost," Fargo agreed.

"I propose we pick up the pace and leave it far behind." With that, the general used his spurs.

Fargo did likewise but he couldn't help thinking that riding faster was an invite to trouble. For one thing, faster meant louder, making it easier for whoever was following them.

For half a mile they pressed steadily on, until the general came to a stop and rose in the stirrups with his ear to the swamp. "We've done it. I haven't heard the thing in a while."

Neither had Fargo but that didn't raise his hopes much that they were out of danger.

"I just remembered," Canton said. "There's an old hunting lodge not far from here. It used to belong to those Petries I was telling you about."

"So?"

"So we'll stop there and let the horses rest. Perhaps put some coffee on to help keep me awake the rest of the night."

Fargo wondered if there was more to it. One minute the general was fired up to push on. Now he wanted to stop for coffee?

They came to where a ribbon of trail led off into the morass, the first they had come across since leaving Haven.

"I don't know about straying off the road," Fargo said.

"Nonsense. I know exactly what I'm doing."

High reeds hemmed them. A misstep would plunge them into the swamp, yet the general treated the danger with disdain.

"I remember this trail as if it were yesterday. I was friends with Aaron Petrie and we'd come out here on occasion."

"No one has been here in a while," was Fargo's hunch.

"Probably not. Like I said, they lost their fortune and went from being the lords of the county to just another penniless clan."

"What happened to your friend?"

"Aaron? The last I heard, he'd gone off to Saint Louis to start over. His father and mother and sister stayed. I lost contact and don't know what became of them."

The trail widened and the reeds gave way to open ground. The solid kind that Fargo liked. An arrow's flight off heavy forest grew.

In between stood the hunting lodge. Fashioned from logs, and with glass windows, it looked to have weathered the time well.

"I'll be damned," General Canton said. "It's exactly as I remember it."

A clearing that once surrounded the lodge was overgrown with weeds. They rode to a hitch rail and dismounted.

"You know," Canton said, "it might do to spend the night here. Get some sleep and head out at first light."

"I thought you were worried that someone is after the troop report," Fargo mentioned.

"Would you rather they caught up with us out in the open?" Canton regarded the lodge with a smile. "Militarily, our advantage is that we know they're after us but they don't know that we know. We'll lure them into our gun sights and put an end to it."

"You're the general," Fargo said. He reached for the Henry to shuck it from the scabbard and happened to glance at one of the windows.

A face was staring back at him.

13

It was there and it was gone but there was no denying Fargo saw it. "General Canton," he said, leveling the Henry.

Canton was staring back the way they came. "Yes? What is it?"

"Someone is in there."

"Unlikely," Canton said. "It's my understanding the family hasn't used the place in years." He moved to the door. "But then again, look at this."

The door hung partway open.

"Let me go first," Fargo advised.

"I don't require nursemaiding." Canton drew a revolver and pushed the door with his boot.

Fargo came right behind. He dimly made out furniture. There was a strong musty smell, and complete quiet.

"I'll see if I can get a lamp to work," General Canton said.

Fargo stayed near the door to keep an eye on their horses. He was loath to leave them untended.

Noises from across the room indicated the general had found a lamp. A lucifer flared, and then a second, and a small flame licked the air.

"This one does."

The flame grew and light spread, illuminating what once must have been a grandly furnished room; rugs covered the floor, the tables and chairs and settees were the best money could buy, paintings hung on the walls. So did the stuffed trophies of a large black bear, a buck with a ten-point rack, and the head of a cougar snarling fiercely forever.

"It's something, isn't it?" General Canton said. "If I had the money, I'd buy this place and restore it."

"We should look around," Fargo suggested. To find whoever had been staring out at them.

"Let's try this," Canton said, and to Fargo's dismay, he threw back his head and shouted, "Is anyone here? This is General Thaddeus Canton. We won't harm you. Show yourself, if you would." To Fargo he said, "That should do it."

No one answered.

"Hmmph," the general said. "I guess we'll have to search, after all."

Just then the Ovaro whinnied.

"Hold on," Fargo said, and hurried out.

Riders were coming. They made no attempt at stealth, and the rustling of the reeds and the thud of hooves showed that they were almost there.

General Canton had followed and was still holding the lamp. "Who can it be at this ungodly hour?"

"Put that behind the door," Fargo said.

"Eh?"

"The lamp," Fargo said. "We're perfect targets."

"Oh. Certainly."

The light faded and Fargo moved to a deep shadow just as a pair of figures on horseback appeared. To his surprise, he distinguished long, flowing hair, and flowing garments, as well.

"Good God," Canton said. "They're women."

The pair came to the hitch rail and Fargo stepped out. Both ladies smiled and one leaned on her saddle horn.

"Remember us?" Belinda asked him.

"It has been hellacious trying to catch up to you," Adelade said, and swiped at a strand of hair.

"You know these two?" General Canton asked.

"We've met," Fargo said, "at the inn."

"What on earth are they doing here?"

"Why don't you ask us, sugar?" Belinda said. "He doesn't know."

Adelade made another swipe at the strand over her face. "We were told that you're bound for New Orleans, Mr. Smith, and we have to get there just as soon as we can."

"So we thought we would ask you if we could tag along," Belinda took up the account. "We were under the impression you had only just left the inn and assumed we could catch up quickly, but what with the road and the dark and all, well, here we are." She smiled sweetly.

"I don't believe it," Canton said. "It must have been unnerving, coming so far in the dark."

Fargo didn't believe their account, either, but for a different reason. For the time being he kept it to himself.

"May we climb down and join you?" Adelade requested. "Because I have to tell you. I'm about ready to fall off my horse, I'm so tired."

"By all means, ladies, by all means," General Canton said, and moved to help them dismount.

"What is this place?" Belinda wanted to know.

Canton related a little of its history while helping with their bags. As they filed past Fargo, Belinda reached out and caressed his chin.

"What's with you, handsome? You've hardly said a word."

"Cat got your tongue?" Adelade teased.

The general set their bags on the floor and brought the lamp over to a table. "There now. This is right cozy."

"I wouldn't say that," Belinda said. She was gazing at the trophies. "Those animal heads make me uneasy."

"She can be squeamish at times," Adelade said.

"You needn't worry," General Canton said, and joked, "It's not as if they can bite you."

"It's the spookiness," Belinda said.

"I still can't believe that you came all this way," Canton brought it up again.

"We received word that my mother is ill," Adelade said. "The next stage from the inn isn't until the day after tomorrow so we figured to get there sooner by traveling with you."

"How fortunate for us," Canton said. "And rest assured," he added, giving Fargo a pointed look, "we'll be perfect gentlemen."

"That's comforting to know," Belinda said, "but there's no need to be fanatical about it."

Both Southern belles, and the general, laughed.

Fargo didn't share in their mirth. Plainly, Canton was smitten; so much for keeping his mind on the mission.

The general went to the hearth and opened the lid to a woodbox. "Why, look at this. There's plenty for a fire. What do you say, my dears? Would it make you more comfortable?"

"It certainly would," Adelade said. "There's nothing more cheering than a fireplace with a fire."

"I'm surprised our scout didn't think of it first," Canton said. "He's the one with a reputation for being so gallant."

"You wouldn't know it to look at him, standing there so quietly," Belinda said.

"He wasn't this way at the inn," Adelade said.

"You must forgive him, ladies," Canton said. "He thinks we're in danger and is acting accordingly."

"Danger from what?" Belinda asked.

"The Night Terror," Canton said.

The man-beast wasn't Fargo's only concern. To one side of the fireplace was a doorway. And peering out at them was the same face as before.

14

This time Fargo saw the face clearly. Which was why he didn't snap the Henry to his shoulder or do anything threatening. Instead, he said, "You can come out now if you want."

"What was that?" General Canton said. "Who can come out?"

A woman stepped timidly into the room. She was somewhere between twenty and thirty, with a face so pale, she must never step foot outside during the day. Her hair was nearly white, which made her look older than she was. A faded dress and shoes long out of fashion added to the illusion.

"What have we here?" Canton said.

Belinda and Adelade swooped and spun, their hands to their handbags. "Who the devil?" the former exclaimed.

"I believe I know her," General Canton said. "It's little Eldrida Petrie, all grown up."

The pale woman looked at them fearfully. "What are you doing here?" she anxiously asked. "You shouldn't be."

"Howdy to you, too, missy," Belinda said.

"Eldrida?" General Canton said. "Don't you recognize me? I used to play with your brother, Aaron, when we were boys."

"He left," Eldrida said. "He was smart."

"How is your mother faring?" Canton asked. "I remember she used to serve us the most delicious cookies."

"Dead," Eldrida said. "She's dead."

"I'm sorry to hear that. And your father?"

"Dead. He's dead, too."

"You poor girl," Canton said.

"There's just me now, and the house and this lodge and the other place. But I don't dare go near the house or that one."

"What one? And why not? Aren't they still in the family?"

Eldrida glanced out the window and wrung her hands. "You shouldn't be here. You really shouldn't."

"Why do you keep saying that?" Adelade said.

"Do you live here at the lodge?" General Canton asked.

Eldrida nodded.

"And here we are, intruding in your home," Canton said. "No wonder you're so upset."

"It's not that. . . ." Eldrida stopped.

"I do apologize," the general said. "But we needed a place to stop for the night. And, too, I was curious about something your brother told me once."

Eldrida gasped and her hand rose to her throat. "What about?"

"I think you know. I would like to ask you if it's true. He said that—" The general got no further.

Uttering a low cry, Eldrida bolted through the doorway.

Belinda started to go after her but Adelade grabbed her arm.

"Let her go. She's just some half-crazed local. She has nothing to do with us."

"I suppose," Belinda said.

Fargo stepped to the door. The room beyond was black as pitch. "Eldrida?" he said, cautiously edging forward.

Out of the blackness came a soft, "Leave me be."

"We will if you want us to but you're welcome to join us," Fargo tried.

"You don't know what you're doing. If you have any sense you'll go before it's too late. Your horses . . ." Again she stopped.

"What about them?"

"You might as well start a bonfire."

"I don't understand," Fargo said.

"Just go. Please. I don't want more blood on my hands."

Fargo thought he heard a low sob. "We'll put coffee on and you can have some if you want."

"You're fools," Eldrida said bitterly.

Fargo backed out.

"Well?" General Canton said.

"She wants to be alone."

"That's too bad. I'd like to ask her some questions. Given her behavior, I'm beginning to think I'm right."

"About what?" Adelade asked.

"It's not anything I can talk about. It was imparted to me in confidence and I must honor my promise not to tell another living soul." General Canton turned to the hearth and set to kindling a fire.

"I'll fetch our bedrolls," Fargo said.

"If you would be so kind," Canton said. "And my saddlebags while you're at it."

"I'll get ours," Belinda said to her companion.

Fargo was almost to the door but stopped so she could precede him. As she went by she grinned and lightly ran the tip of her finger across his cheek. "What was that for?"

"You're so darned good-looking, a girl just wants to touch you," Belinda said playfully.

The muggy air and the darkness enveloped them like a humid glove. As she moved to her horse she remarked, "It's a stroke of luck, us being thrown together like this."

"Is it?" Fargo said. He was listening to the sounds of the swamp and the forest. All seemed normal.

"We have the entire night together." Belinda looked at him over her saddle. "To do whatever we'd like."

"Did you have something in mind?"

"Don't play innocent with me," Belinda said, chuckling. "I saw how you looked at us back at the inn. You practically devoured me with your eyes."

The Ovaro picked that moment to turn its head in the direction of the road and stamp a front hoof a couple of times.

"What's gotten into your animal?" Belinda asked.

"Something is out there."

"So long as it's not the Night Terror," Belinda said, and laughed.

"It doesn't worry you?"

"Everyone says it only kills men, remember?"

Fargo suddenly realized someone was standing almost at his elbow. He turned, thinking it must be Adelade, but it was Eldrida Petrie, her hands clasped tight, her face ghostly.

"Whoever told you that is wrong," Eldrida said to Belinda. "If it gets ahold of you, it will wring your head from your neck." She looked at Fargo. "Not one of you is safe."

15

"Aren't you the gruesome little thing?" Belinda said, laughing. "Spare me your horror tales, missy. I can take care of myself, I'll have you know."

"You only think you can," Eldrida said.

Fargo was interested in something else. "You called the Night Terror an 'it'? You don't think it's a man?"

"Not the way you mean, no."

"And what in blue blazes does *that* mean, dearie?" Belinda said. "Either it's a man or an animal."

"That's what you think."

Belinda slid her bedroll under her arm and moved to Adelade's mount. "You like being mysterious. Is that it?"

"You don't know," Eldrida said.

"I know you're damned silly," Belinda said. "Living in this old place all by your lonesome with no one for company except stuffed animal heads. And now you're trying to scare us into leaving."

"That's not it at all."

"Oh, please. I wasn't born yesterday." Belinda untied her friend's bedroll and held it under her arm. "I'd feel sorry for you if you weren't so pathetic. You're a hermit in a dress, is what you are. A little girl scared of the real world, hiding out in the middle of nowhere."

"Stop calling me little."

"Or what? You'll use bad language?" Belinda laughed and went past them, saying to Fargo, "Watch yourself. Little miss scared-of-everything will have you jumping at your shadow if you're not careful."

"She's mean," Eldrida said as the door closed behind her.

"She's more than that," Fargo said, "but she has a point. Why do you stay here alone?"

"It's the only way. The only safe way."

"There you go again," Fargo said. "Talking in riddles."

"I don't mean to." Eldrida stared at the benighted forest and her voice quavered as she said softly, "It's the horror of it all. I never could deal with violence very well. Been that way since I was little."

"About the Night Terror?" Fargo prompted.

"I've said all I'm going to. More than I should, actually." Eldrida placed her hand on his arm. "Listen to me. You owe it to yourself and these others to persuade them to go before it's too late."

"It wouldn't do any good for me to try," Fargo said. "They have to play it out to the end."

"Play what out?"

"Their game of cat and mouse."

"And you say I talk in riddles?" Eldrida said accusingly. "Can't you make them go?"

"They have the right to do as they please."

"Not when it gets them killed." Eldrida did more hand wringing. "I'm wasting my time, aren't I? None of you will mount up and go even though your lives depend on it."

"So long as the gent I'm with stays, I stay."

"You're fools *and* simpletons," Eldrida said angrily, then put a hand to her forehead. "I'm losing my temper. It's not fair."

"To who?"

"To you, of course. You can't help being ignorant of the facts. Although if you weren't, my instincts tell me you'd stay anyway." Eldrida raised her pale face to the stars. "Oh, whatever am I to do?"

"Let me treat you to some coffee."

"Why not? You're the first company I've had in a coon's age, and of all of them, I like you the best. Just promise me something."

"If I can."

"Don't hold it against me later that I couldn't convince you to leave."

A strange request, Fargo thought, but then Eldrida was a mite peculiar. "I promise that if the Night Terror kills me, I won't blame you."

He intended it as a joke but Eldrida Petrie closed her eyes and swayed slightly and then looked at him with an intensity that was unnerving. "Do you ever feel trapped?" She didn't let him answer. "I do. Every minute of every day. I should have left when Aaron did. I should have gotten as far away as I could so I wouldn't have to live in fear anymore. But you can't run away from who you are, can you?"

Fargo didn't know what to say to that. She wasn't being very clear. "I suppose not," he hedged.

"It was done before I was born yet it has haunted me since the day we first found out."

"Found out what?"

Eldrida didn't seem to hear him. She was gazing into the distance, or perhaps into her past. "When it's your own family, what can you do? Have nothing to do with them ever again? Not if you love them. Don't you see?"

"No."

"Who can say why things like that happen?" she went on, more to herself than to him. "Is it an act of God? Does the Devil have a hand in it, like some in my family thought? Is it the mark of Cain?" She sadly shook her head. "My whole life has been ruined because of it. My grandmother used to say we were cursed and maybe she was right. Maybe that's all there is to it."

"To what?"

Just then, from the depths of the swamp, rose the inhuman wail Fargo had heard before. Unlike any cry made by human or beast, it rose and fell like the swells on an ocean. Sorrowful, yet somehow fierce, it was both a cry of torment and a scream of defiance.

Eldrida gasped and gripped her throat with both hands. "There! Do you hear! He's abroad again."

"Before you called the thing an 'it' and now you call it 'he.' Which is it?" Fargo said.

The distant cry faded.

Eldrida gave a low sob and turned to go back in but stopped. "Oh. Look at that. Isn't it pretty?"

The front window was aglow with light from the fire the general had started in the hearth.

"I miss pretty things," Eldrida said. "For far too long, I'm sorry to say, my life has been ugly."

With that puzzling comment, she went in.

Fargo stayed outside a while, listening. The wail wasn't repeated. It had been far off and he deemed it unlikely they had anything to worry about. But the Night Terror wasn't the only danger.

This whole affair had become too complicated. There was the thing in the swamp, and the spy business. Give him the West, where a man usually knew who his enemies were.

With a toss of his head, Fargo moved to rejoin the rest. From here on out he must stay sharp if he didn't want to end up like Jerrod Wilkes or with a dagger in his back.

16

With the crackling fire and coffee on to brew and spreading its aroma, the hunting lodge became downright cozy.

General Canton had claimed an easy chair and was puffing on a cigar. Belinda and Adelade huddled on a settee, whispering every now and then.

Eldrida had disappeared.

Fargo leaned on the wall next to the front window, where he could keep an eye on their horses. He'd been holding the Henry in the crook of his right arm but now he switched it to the left.

"You should learn to relax more," General Canton told him with a smile. "Like me."

"I'll relax when you're in New Orleans."

Adelade stirred and grinned and said, "What are you, handsome? His protector?"

"I doubt he even needs one," Belinda said, "a strong man like Mr. Smith."

"Why, thank you, my dear," the general said. "It warms this old heart to think you think so."

"You're not that old," Belinda said.

"And you certainly look fit," Adelade said.

"I thank you again," General Canton said. "I admit I take pride in staying vigorous."

Fargo thought of some of the potbellied officers he'd known.

"I don't mean to boast," Canton went on, "but I daresay I'm as hearty and hale as a man half my age."

"Let's hope you stay that way," Fargo tried to remind him to keep his mind on the matter at hand. Canton had been buttering up to the ladies since they got there. It didn't bode well.

"I have you to watch over me," the general said, smiling, "and I have this." He opened his coat to reveal a revolver in a shoulder holster.

"I feel safe with you two here," Adelade said.

"So do I," Belinda was quick to throw in.

"No one is safe," declared the pale figure of Eldrida Petrie as she floated into the room on soundless soles. "I wish you would realize that before it's too late."

"Not you again," Belinda said.

Eldrida walked over to Fargo. "You're the most sensible. Please. Before it's too late. Convince them to go."

"We're not going anywhere, my dear," General Canton said. "We're safer in here than out there. At least until daybreak."

Eldrida sighed and gazed out the window. "I've tried my best. It's on your shoulders now." She jerked her head higher. "Who are they?"

Fargo looked, and swore. While he'd been distracted, three riders had emerged from the tall reeds and were halfway to the hunting lodge. "Company coming," he said, and hurried out.

The lead rider plastered a smile on his face. "Don't shoot, mister. It's only us."

Wayland, Hosiah, and Abimelech Wilkes held their hands where Fargo could see them as they rode up and drew rein.

"See? We're harmless," Abimelech said.

Fargo knew better. "You'd better have a damn good reason."

"Eh?" Wayland said.

"For following us."

Before they could respond, General Canton appeared, his revolver in hand. Behind him came Belinda and Adelade.

"What do we have here?" Wayland said, and whistled in appreciation. "Where did you lovelies come from?"

"The same place you did," Belinda said. "Our mother's womb."

"I love a gal who talks dirty," Wayland said.

"Enough of that," Canton snapped. "As Mr. Fargo said, you'd best have an explanation I'll accept for your presence."

"Listen to you," Abimelech said. "It's a free country, ain't it?"

"Not tonight," Fargo said.

Hosiah looked at Wayland. "Just tell them. It's not as if we've done anythin' worth bein' shot over."

"I don't see as I ought to, but, hell," Wayland said, and grinned down at Fargo. "I had me one of my feelin's."

"Your what?"

"Some folks would call them hunches but they're more than that. Every now and then I get a powerful feelin' about somethin' or other and they usually turn out to be right. I had one about you."

Adelade laughed. "Next you'll be telling us that you read palms and tell the future in crystal balls."

"I'm serious, woman," Wayland said. "I've had these feelin's since I was a kid. They just come over me. I had one about buckskin, here, when he told us about his run-in with the Night Terror."

"Talk plainly, man," General Canton said.

"We're after that critter for what it did to our cousin. And when your pard told us about how he found our cousin's head, I got the feelin' he was holdin' somethin' back. That he didn't tell the whole truth."

Fargo was amazed. Yes, he'd held something back—that he was on a secret mission for the army.

"So when the clerk told us that the two of you had lit out, suddenlike, I figured it might have somethin' to do with the Night Terror, that maybe you were goin' after it yourselves. So we came after you."

"You couldn't be further from the truth," General Canton said.

"Why else would you be here at the old huntin' lodge if not to hunt it?" Wayland countered, and gestured at the front window. "Truth to tell, I'd plumb forgotten about the place until we caught sight of the light from the road."

"Trust me," Canton said, "when I tell you we have no interest in whatever killed your cousin."

"Bumpkins, all three of them," Belinda said.

"Watch your mouth," Wayland growled. To the general he said, "As for you, you're not one of us no more. You left the backwoods to be a high muck-a-muck in the army. I'd no more trust you than I would a patent medicine man."

"Here now," Canton said indignantly.

"You've forgotten how it is with us," Wayland said. "The code we live by."

"You have a code?" Adelade said, and snickered.

"That's right, lady," Wayland said. "It's all about blood. Kin counts for everythin'. We stick by our own, come hell or high water. When one of us is in need, the rest lend a hand. When one gets into a scrape, the rest fight with him. And when one of us is killed, we kill the killer."

"How dashing of you," Belinda said dryly.

"What do you know, bitch? You're not from these parts. All you've likely ever cared about is your own hides. You don't know what it means to care about somethin' that's more important than you are."

"Like hell we don't," Adelade bristled, and would have said more except that Belinda grabbed her wrist and shook her head.

"Forget the women. They're not important," Hosiah said. He

pointed at Fargo. "What will it be, mister? Are you goin' to let us in or do we make camp out here?"

"No, don't do that," said a new voice, and around the corner came Eldrida Petrie. She moved in a way that made it seem she was floating over the ground, and with her hair and her pale face, Fargo didn't blame the Wilkes brothers for giving starts of surprise.

"God Almighty!" Abimelech blurted.

"Where did she come from?" Hosiah said.

"Who are you, gal?" Wayland asked.

General Canton held out an arm for Eldrida to come closer to him but she stayed where she was. "Permit me to introduce Miss Petrie, the owner of this lodge."

"Well then," Wayland said with a sly smile, "she has rightful say in whether we come in or not. What about it, little lady?"

"You can't stay outside," Eldrida said, gazing fearfully about. "If it comes, you wouldn't stand a prayer."

"You're expectin' the Night Terror to pay a visit?" Hosiah said.

"There's no predicting what it will do," Eldrida answered. "The only thing you can say for sure is that if it finds us, it will kill us. Each and every one of us. Including me, ironically enough."

"Why ironical?" Wayland asked.

Instead of responding, Eldrida wheeled and melted around the corner as soundlessly as she had appeared.

"That gal is plumb weird," Abimelech said.

Wayland chuckled. "Between you and me, brother, I have me one of my feelin's there's a lot worse to come."

It didn't help Fargo's peace of mind that he had the same feeling.

17

Hardly anyone said a word.

Fargo was at his post at the window. General Canton was in the easy chair, smoking. Belinda and Adelade had spread their bedrolls near the fireplace and were sitting on their blankets.

As for the Wilkes brothers, Hosiah and Abimelech were on the settee, Wayland on the floor beside them. For the past half an hour they had been passing a flask back and forth.

"I can't say I approve," General Canton remarked as Hosiah took a swig. "No good can come of being drunk."

"Who asked you?" Wayland retorted. "And a few sips ain't hardly goin' to affect us much."

"We need our heads clear for the Night Terror," Abimelech said.

Hosiah nodded. "We don't aim to end up like Jerrod."

"You should be out hunting the thing," Belinda said. "Unless you expect it to come down the chimney."

Adelade laughed.

"Why are you two so all-fired set to get rid of us?" Wayland asked. "We ain't treated you with any disrespect."

"We don't trust you," Belinda said.

"Why not? Have we so much as laid a finger on you?" Wayland angrily demanded. "We have not. You ask me, you two ladies are up to no good."

"Another of your hunches?" Belinda said.

"No," Wayland said. "I just don't like you."

"Enough bickering, if you please," General Canton said. "Since we're forced to spend the night together, we should try to get along."

"Says you," Wayland said.

Fargo could use some air. Hefting the Henry, he went out and around to the side of the lodge. The forest was a stone's throw off, a black wall of vegetation. An owl hooted. Farther away, a deer bleated in alarm. He continued his circuit until he came to a rear door.

It was wide open.

"What the hell?" Fargo said. Anyone could sneak inside and

they'd be none the wiser. He reached for the latch to close it and a slender hand touched his wrist.

"Please don't." Eldrida Petrie acquired pale form and substance. "I've been keeping watch. If he shows up, I'll warn you."

"So this is where you got to."

"I can see without being seen. Most nights, I stand here until near dawn. I can't hardly sleep, anyway."

Fargo noticed that she hadn't removed her hand. "It must get lonely."

"It used to," Eldrida said. "I would cry all the time. But not anymore. I've accepted my responsibility."

"How are you responsible for the Night Terror?"

"When you throw a rock in a pond, there are ripples, are there not? In my case the rock was thrown before I was born but I'm still one of the ripples."

"You and your mysteries," Fargo said.

Her grip on his arm tightened. "You could save them, you know."

"How?"

"March inside and demand they leave at gunpoint. Shoot one if you have to, in order to convince them. In an hour you can be far away."

"They won't take kindly to being told what to do," Fargo mentioned. Half in jest he added, "Odds are I'd have to shoot more than one."

"Shoot as many as it takes."

"I didn't reckon you were so bloodthirsty," Fargo teased. "Will you do the burying for me?"

Eldrida said harshly, "Do you think this is a joke? They'll all of them die if it comes."

"We're back to 'it,'" Fargo said. "What makes you so sure it will?"

"It comes here from time to time, searching. . . ." Eldrida averted her face.

"Searching for what?"

"For me. It blames everyone but especially my family. With my brother gone, I'm all who's left." Eldrida frowned.

"If you ever make any damn sense I'll whoop for joy." Fargo shouldered the Henry. "It's been nice talking to you," he said sarcastically.

"Wait," Eldrida suddenly whispered. "Listen."

Fargo heard it at the same time she did, a faint crackling as if something huge was plowing through dense growth. He faced the forest and tried to pinpoint the direction but the fickle wind kept shifting.

"It's him!"

It could be, Fargo reflected. It could also just as well be a bear or a horse or even a stray cow, for all he knew.

"Do you believe me now that he's coming?"

"You're only guessing."

Eldrida smacked her palm with a fist. "Consarn you, anyhow. Why won't you believe me? What will it take to convince you?"

"To see it with my own eyes," Fargo said.

"You only see it when it wants you to. You only hear it when it's not stalking you. The first you'll know it's there is when its fingers are around your throat."

"Fingers," Fargo said. "You said fingers."

"Will you quit quibbling over what it is?" Eldrida said. "The important thing is that . . ." She stopped, and gasped.

A gust of wind brought the crackling and snapping. Was it Fargo's imagination or were the sounds louder than before? And if they were louder, they had to be closer. He didn't realize he was holding his breath until the sounds ceased and he let it out.

"I warned you," Eldrida said. "As God is my witness, I warned you." Without any warning she shut the door in his face and he heard the rasp of a bolt.

Fargo was tired of her antics. Wheeling, he strode to the front, gave the Ovaro a pat, and went in.

Nothing had changed. Canton still smoked, the Wilkeses were still sharing a flask, Belinda and Adelade were still by the fire.

"Anything?" the general asked.

"Branches breaking, far off."

"Could be anything." Canton puffed and blew a smoke ring. "I suppose one of us should turn in while the other stands guard."

"Why don't you both get some sleep?" Wayland said. "We don't mind standin' watch a spell."

"That's kind of you," Canton said, "but he and I have a pact that one or the other must always be awake."

"That's fine for when the two of you are alone," Belinda said. "But you have us to help you."

Fargo didn't trust her any more than he did the Wilkes brothers. "Mr. Smith and I like to do things ourselves." To Canton he said, "You sleep first."

"I won't argue," the general said. "I'm too bushed." Rising, he moved past Fargo and spread out his bedroll next to the wall. "So no one can get at me without you noticing," he explained.

"Why would anyone want to?" Belinda asked.

"No telling," was Canton's reply.

Fargo thought that was remarkably careless but the ladies didn't pry deeper and the Wilkeses didn't seem to care.

Adelade stretched and yawned and said, "If he's turning in, we might as well, too. I can't keep my eyes open much longer."

Next it was Hosiah and Abimelech who curled on the floor and drifted off, Hosiah starting to snore almost immediately.

That left Wayland. He'd taken a piece of firewood from the wood-box and was sitting cross-legged, sharpening it to a point with a folding knife. He didn't act tired at all.

Twice Fargo noticed him staring. His wariness increased when Wayland unexpectedly stood and came over to the other side of the window and leaned against the wall.

"Mind if we jaw some?"

"What about?"

"Anything. I can't sleep and I'm bored carvin' on this stick." Wayland held it up. The point was sharp enough to penetrate flesh.

"I'm not much of a talker," Fargo said. He'd never been one of those who flapped their jaws to hear themselves talk.

"Me either, although I can when the occasion calls for it and the occasion calls for it now."

"Oh?"

"Supposin' you tell me what you and Thaddeus, there, are really up to?"

"You should use that knife to trim your nose," Fargo said.

Wayland grinned. "Is that your way of sayin' I'm stickin' it where it don't belong? Fair enough. But I'm beginnin' to think I was wrong about you bein' after the Night Terror."

"If I never see it again, I'll be a happy man."

Wayland glanced out the window and said casually, "I reckon you're about to be sad as hell, then."

"Why?" Fargo said, and looked out.

Between the lodge and the reeds a giant dark shape was hunched over on all fours.

18

"The Night Terror!" Wayland Wilkes hollered, and dashed to his brothers. Drawing his revolver, he bawled, "Up! Get up! The killer of our cousin is right outside."

Fargo snapped the Henry to his shoulder, ready to shoot through the glass if the thing came at them. But Wayland's ruckus caused it to whirl and with astounding speed dart to the reeds and disappear.

The ladies had woken up and were looking around in confusion while General Canton sleepily shook himself and rubbed his eyes.

The Wilkes brothers pounded to the front door and out into the night. They spread out as they moved to where the Night Terror had been standing. Fargo thought they might go into the reeds after it but they had the presence of mind not to.

By then Canton was by Fargo's side, peering out. "Was it really the Terror?"

"I saw it with my own eyes," Fargo said.

"We should go after it, then. I owe it to the people of this community to do what I can to stop the killings."

"Is that why we stopped here?" Fargo had suspected there was more to the general's decision than curiosity.

"I was born and raised here, remember?"

"What about your duty to the government?" Fargo asked quietly so the women wouldn't hear.

"I can do both," Canton said defensively. "With your help."

"What do you want me to do?"

"You're one of the best trackers alive, or so everyone says. Who better to find the thing? And you owe it for that crack on your head. You told me so yourself."

Fargo thought it strange that Canton considered hunting the Night Terror as more important than getting the dispatch pouch to Washington. "You could have told me this at the inn."

Canton shrugged. "Other factors are now in play."

"Such as?"

"I'd rather not say at this time. The important thing is that we can go after the thing in the morning," Canton said.

"Is that your way of asking?"

"I can't order you," Canton said. "It's not army business. But think of the lives we could save."

Fargo was thinking he'd rather be anywhere than at that damn lodge. He was angry, but before he could vent it, the Wilkeses trooped back in.

"The critter got away," Wayland said. "I wanted to go after it but the two yellowbellies I'm with wouldn't."

"Insult us again," Abimelech said. "I dare you."

"It wouldn't be smart to go blunderin' around in the dark," Hosiah said. "We should wait for daylight."

"Perhaps we can join forces," General Canton said. "I'd like to go after it, too."

"Well, now," Wayland said. "We'll have us a regular huntin' party. How about buckskin? Is he taggin' along."

Reluctantly, Fargo said, "I wouldn't miss it."

Belinda rose from her blankets. "What about us? You'd leave us alone while you go traipsin' off to get yourselves killed?"

"You're nothin' to us," Wayland said. "But you're welcome to come along if you're afraid to stay."

"Nothing, are we?" Belinda said archly.

"You have to excuse him," Hosiah said. "He's the youngest and tends to speak his mind without thinkin' first."

"What good would these females be on a hunt?" Abimelech said. "I vote we leave them here."

Adelade said, "I'm not going into the swamp, I'll tell you that. There are snakes and alligators and bogs."

"And the Night Terror," Wayland said.

Fargo heard the Ovaro and another horse nicker and went out the front door.

Almost all the horses were staring at where the reeds met the woods. He could guess why. The Night Terror was circling the hunting lodge.

"Anything?" General Canton said behind him.

"It's being cagey," Fargo said. Whatever "it" was.

The three Wilkes brothers emerged and stood with their heads raised, listening, bloodhounds eager to take up a scent.

"Just one shot at its heart or its head," Wayland said grimly. "That's all I ask."

"And cousin Jerrod will be avenged," Hosiah said.

"You boys must have been very close to him," General Canton remarked.

"We saw him now and again," Abimelech said. "But we weren't as close to him as to some other of our kin."

"Yet here you are," Canton said.

"Blood is blood," Wayland declared.

Fargo wished they would shut up. Their jabber would drown faint sounds the Night Terror might make. "Hush," he said.

"Who are you to tell us to shush?" Abimelech said. "We have a right to talk if we want."

"You can lose teeth, too," Fargo said.

Abimelech balled his fist. "I'd like to see you try. You hit me, my brothers and me will wail on you. You won't take us by surprise like you did at the inn."

"No you won't," Wayland echoed.

General Canton moved between them. "Gentlemen, please. Our adversary is out there. Fighting among ourselves does none of us any good."

"You sure you're a soldier?" Hosiah said.

Wayland laughed. "Fightin' is one of the three joys of life. The others are drinkin' and pokin', and I don't mean with fingers, neither."

Fargo wasn't looking to tangle with them a second time. They were hardheads and nuisances but they weren't bad men at heart.

Just then, from the rear of the hunting lodge, there was a tremendous crash, as of the splintering and rending of wood, and the night was shattered by a fierce howl.

19

"It's the critter!" Wayland Wilkes bawled, and he and his brothers charged off.

Whirling, Fargo ran inside. He almost collided with Belinda and Adelade, who were racing out, and he pushed them out of his way. Crossing the main room, he paused at a narrow hall that led to the back. The light from the fireplace extended only a short way. Beyond, it was black as pitch. "Eldrida?" he called out.

Eldrida Petrie screamed.

Fargo hurtled down the hall. He couldn't see a thing and thrust a hand in front of him. His very next stride, his legs slammed painfully into something in his path, and he tumbled. His head smacked the wall and his elbows were jarred by the impact of hitting the floor. He managed to hold on to the Henry and scrambled to a knee.

Somewhere ahead there was a crash and a rumbling growl.

"No! No!" Eldrida cried. "Please!"

A roar shook the lodge, and she screamed a second time in sheer and utter terror.

"Eldrida!" Fargo groped about and discovered he had tripped over a chair left lying in the middle of the hall. God only knew why. Rising, he advanced cautiously, unwilling to risk another spill with the Terror so close.

From ahead came the whisper of stealthy movement and a low sob.

The black became a gray, thanks to starlight filtering in through what was left of the shattered rear door. Even as Fargo set eyes on it, something huge flew with incredible speed out into the night. He couldn't make out what it was but he did see it bore a pale burden it had flung over a giant shoulder.

"Eldrida!" Fargo fixed a quick bead. As much as he wanted to shoot, he held his fire. He might hit her.

Apparently the Wilkes brothers had no such compunctions. No sooner did the Night Terror burst from the lodge than their rifles boomed.

"No!" Fargo flew outside.

The creature was moving with a swiftness that defied belief, Eldrida flopping against its broad back, her arms dangling.

Wayland, Hosiah, and Abimelech were frantically reloading their single-shot rifles. Quicker than the others, Wayland jerked his long gun to his shoulder. "That son of a bitch is as good as dead."

Fargo didn't yell at him not to shoot. He reached him in two bounds and drove the Henry's stock against Wayland's head. Wayland folded, and Fargo covered the other two to keep them from firing. "No more shooting."

"What the hell?" Abimelech said.

"You might hit the girl."

"What girl?" Hosiah said, and stared after the rapidly retreating forms. "Oh, hell. I didn't see her or I wouldn't have shot."

The Night Terror reached the edge of the forest and stopped. It raised a giant arm and shook it and roared in defiance, then plunged into the undergrowth with its burden.

"Where is it goin' with her?" Hosiah said. "I thought it didn't hurt females."

Wayland groaned.

"How hard did you hit him?" Abimelech said.

Around the corner came General Canton with the two Southern belles. "What happened?" Canton asked. "What did we miss?"

"The thing got Eldrida Petrie," Fargo said. "Look after my horse until I get back." He broke into a run.

"Wait!" Canton said. "What are you doing?"

"What does it look like?" Hosiah said. "He's goin' after it."

"Who cares that it took her?" Belinda hollered. "Good riddance, I say."

Fargo shut them from his mind and focused on the woods. He slowed as he got closer and became aware of someone coming up fast behind him. Stopping, he turned. "What do you want?"

"It's better if there're two of us," Hosiah Wilkes said. "I can cover your back."

Fargo wasn't sure he trusted him but he had no time to waste arguing. "What about your brothers?"

"I told Abimelech to look after Wayland and come join us when they can." Hosiah peered into the rank vegetation. "Where did it get to? I don't hear it."

Neither did Fargo, yet moments ago the thing had been making as much noise as a herd of buffalo.

"Do we or don't we?" Hosiah asked.

Fargo slipped into the growth on cat's feet. The forest had gone unnaturally still. Not so much as a cricket chirped. He sidestepped a low limb that would have snagged his buckskins and went around a log.

Hosiah's woodcraft was exceptional. He made no more sound than Fargo except once when a dry leaf crunched under his foot.

Fargo's skin began to prickle. He had that feeling again of unseen eyes on him. The thing hadn't run off. It had stopped to ambush anyone who came after it. He went a little farther and halted.

Hosiah whispered, "Why did you stop?"

"It's close," Fargo whispered back.

Hosiah swiveled his head one hundred and eighty degrees. Shaking it, he whispered, "I don't see it nowhere."

Fargo needed to be certain. He looked for anything out of the ordinary, any shape that seemed out of place or a silhouette where there shouldn't be one.

Impatient, Hosiah didn't wait. He started forward on his own, poised on the balls of his feet.

Fargo smothered his annoyance. Hosiah probably figured the risk was worth it to save Eldrida but they couldn't help her if they were dead. He opened his mouth to warn Hosiah to wait.

An immense bulk exploded out of nowhere. It was on Hosiah in the bat of an eye, reaching for his neck.

Hosiah fired at near point-blank range. He couldn't have missed yet the Night Terror didn't slow. A massive arm lashed out, knocking the rifle from Hosiah's grasp, while its other hand clamped on to his throat.

Fargo fired at the thing's chest, worked the Henry's lever, fired again. It had no effect. He was centering the muzzle on the creature's head when the Night Terror roared and hurled Hosiah at him. Fargo tried to dodge but he was bowled over. Worried the thing would pounce while he was down, he shoved onto his knees.

Just as a gigantic foot swept at his face.

20

Fargo shifted and bore the force of the kick on his shoulder but it still felt like he had been slammed into by a ten-ton boulder. Catapulted into the air, he struck a tree.

The impact jarred him to his marrow. His vision swam and he came close to blacking out.

A whimper brought him out of the descending veil.

"Eldrida?" he croaked, struggling to stand. He'd lost the Henry but miraculously his Colt was still in his holster and he fumbled it out and gazed dazedly about. "Where are you?"

The whimper was repeated, but fainter. The crackle of brush told him she was being borne off.

"Damn," Fargo said, and collapsed onto his hands and knees. His shoulder throbbed, and his senses roiled as if he had been spun in a circle for minutes on end.

A strangled cough let him know he wasn't the only one to survive the attack.

"Hosiah?"

There was no answer.

"Hosiah? Answer me."

"Can't hardly breathe. . . ."

Through sheer force of will, Fargo heaved upright. He staggered in the direction of the backwoodsman's voice and found him on his back, clutching his throat and wheezing. "How bad?"

"The thing damn near crushed it," Hosiah got out. "Give me a minute."

Fargo needed a few himself. He cast about for his Henry, afraid he might not find it. The gleam of starlight off the brass receiver brought a twitch of a smile. He picked it up and brushed it off and shoved the Colt into his holster.

More crackling and crunching heralded the arrival of the others. All of them: General Canton, Wayland and Abimelech, Belinda and Adelade.

Canton came to Fargo and unwittingly gripped him by his hurt shoulder. "Are you all right? Where is it? We heard shots."

Wincing, Fargo pulled loose. "It got away."

"And the Petrie woman?"

"It took her."

Wayland and Abimelech were helping Hosiah to his feet. "You should have stayed with us," the former told him.

"Look at you," Abimelech said. "You damned near got yourself killed."

"I shot it," Hosiah rasped with an effort. "Hit it, too. I know I did."

"Same here," Fargo said.

"And didn't kill it?" General Canton said skeptically.

"I know," Fargo said. It sounded preposterous. He stared into the depths of the forest, thinking of the pale woman who had been hiding from the thing, only to have her worst fear come true. "In the morning I'm going after them," he announced.

"Not alone, you're not," Hosiah said.

"Count me in, too," Canton said.

"Hold on," Belinda spoke up. "We brought this up before. You'd leave us alone and defenseless while you go riding off to rescue that little witch?"

"You don't endear us with comments like that," General Canton said.

"She's right, though," Adelade said. "Some of you should stay."

"Don't look at us," Wayland said. "We owe that critter." He turned toward Fargo. "Speakin' of owin', that was low of you, hittin' me when I wasn't lookin'."

"You might have shot Eldrida," Fargo said.

"Then you should have swatted my gun," Wayland said. "You didn't need to damn near take my head off."

"You wouldn't miss it," Fargo said.

"What the hell is that supposed to mean?"

"Leave it be," Hosiah said.

"You're takin' his side?" Wayland said, incredulous.

"He did what he had to," Hosiah said. "I'd have done the same if'n I'd seen the thing was carryin' her. But we're so worked up to spill its blood, we didn't look close enough."

"It ain't right, you not sidin' with your own brother," Wayland said.

"It sure ain't," Abimelech said.

"Both of you listen," Hosiah said. "However we've got to do it, we're goin' to kill that critter for killin' our kin. Fargo, here, can help us. So I don't want to hear about sides."

"Well, still," Abimelech said.

"Am I the oldest or am I the oldest?" Hosiah said.

"You are," Wayland said sulkily.

"Then we do as I say and I say we partner with the scout and get it done."

Fargo wasn't anxious to have them at his side. By the same token, their help might come in handy. And their guns definitely would. "I'll let you come along on one condition."

"Name it," Hosiah said.

"You do as I say."

"Hell," Wayland said.

"He's a damn fine tracker, boy," General Canton said. "You can trust him. I do."

"I'm not you," Wayland said.

"If I'm willing to let him take charge, you should be, too."

"Means squat to me," Wayland said. "To me you're just Thaddeus from the bayou puttin' on airs."

"Your attitude is tiresome," General Canton said.

"Enough squabblin'," Hosiah said to Wayland. "It's settled. Fargo leads and we follow."

Wayland muttered something but fell silent.

"Don't worry about me, big brother," Abimelech said to Hosiah. "I'll do whatever you say. I always do, don't I?"

"I'm glad that's settled," Canton said.

"Like Hades it is," Belinda said angrily, her hands on her hips. "You still haven't said what you aim to do about Adelade and me. Surely you're not going to leave us here by ourselves?"

"In the morning you can head for New Orleans," Fargo said.

"By our lonesome? In swamp country? Are you out of your mind? Or don't you care what happens to us?"

"No one asked you to follow us," Fargo said.

"That's harsh," Adelade retorted.

"Yes, it is," General Canton said. "Very well, ladies. I'll stay with you while Fargo and the Wilkeses go after the Night Terror and Miss Petrie."

"No," Fargo said.

"No?"

"You're coming with me," Fargo said. "Abimelech can stay with them."

Abimelech, Adelade, and Belinda all said "What?" at the same time.

"Why Abimelech?" Hosiah asked.

"I have my reasons," Fargo said. He couldn't very well tell them about the important information the general was carrying.

"I don't like it," Wayland said.

Abimelech was looking at the Southern belles as if he couldn't believe his good fortune. "I don't mind. They're right pretty."

"If you so much as try to lay a finger on us . . ." Belinda said.

"I'd never, ma'am," Abimelech said. "Our ma taught us to respect womanhood."

"Wonderful," Adelade said.

"It's settled, then," General Canton. "At first light we hunt the creature down."

"If it doesn't kill you first," Belinda said.

21

The aroma of fresh coffee filled the lodge.

Fargo inserted a sixth cartridge into the cylinder of his Colt and twirled the revolver into his holster. He made sure the Henry's tubular magazine was full.

Outside the window, the black of night was giving way to the gray of predawn. Soon the sun would be up.

Over in a chair the general was enjoying a last smoke.

The Wilkeses were huddled in a corner, talking in low tones.

Fargo went to the fireplace to fill his tin cup. He ignored the barbed stares of Belinda and Adelade.

"I hope you're happy," the former said.

"Leaving us with that boy," said Adelade.

"Stay close to the lodge and you'll be fine," Fargo said. "I doubt the thing will come back."

"Who can say what it will do?" Belinda said.

Fargo went over to Canton. "Stay close to me today. We can't have anything happen to you."

Canton motioned with his cigar. "You must think me reckless to put my life at hazard when I should be hurrying to Washington. But if hostilities do break out, it won't be for months." He scowled. "Plus there's Miss Petrie. What sort of man would I be if I didn't make an attempt to rescue her?"

"Before, you said we stopped here because this is where you were raised and you should do what you could to stop the killings."

"Are you suggesting I'm concocting excuses? I assure you I'm sincere." Canton fingered his cigar. "I have a philosophy I've always lived by. Simply put, it's this." He paused. "A man does what he has to. What is right for each circumstance. Were I to turn my back on Miss Petrie, I would be the most abominable coward."

Fargo admired his sentiments. They were a lot alike in that respect. "What if we find her dead?"

"Will I give up and head for the Capitol? No. I'm determined to see this through to the end. Which reminds me. Should something happen to me, I'm counting on you to see that the report gets to the president."

Wayland intruded on their whispers by saying, "The sun is comin' up. How much longer before we head out?"

"Five minutes," Fargo said.

A blazing ball sat on the eastern rim of the world when Fargo forked leather. The air was crisp, almost cool, but would soon become hot and muggy. The gators and frogs had fallen silent. Songbirds warbled in the forest but they would soon fall silent, too.

The women and Abimelech watched them ride off. Abimelech waved and hollered, "Be careful, brothers."

The women looked fit to spit nails.

Fargo led the way. No sooner had he entered the trees than he found what he was looking for. The Night Terror hadn't made any effort at throwing pursuers off. He or it had plowed through the vegetation like a bull buffalo gone amok, flattening grass and breaking limbs and tearing through thickets as if they didn't exist, leaving a wide swath in its wake.

"God Almighty," Hosiah said. "What sort of critter can do this? Our hounds have chased some mighty big bears and those bears didn't tear up half as much vegetation as this thing."

"It's unfortunate you don't have your hounds with you now," General Canton remarked.

"Dogs won't go after it," Wayland said. "The few times it's been tried, they break off and won't budge."

"Almost as if it's the Devil himself," Hosiah said.

"Don't be ridiculous," said General Canton. "This thing is flesh and blood, just like you and me."

The crushed undergrowth took them another hundred yards or so, and suddenly the trail ended at a wall of seemingly undisturbed greenery.

"What the hell?" Wayland said.

Fargo climbed down. There had to be tracks. Something as huge and heavy as the Terror couldn't vanish into thin air. Bending, he scoured the ground and smiled when he found slightly bent stems. He parted them with his hand, and there in the dirt was an imprint. Not of an entire foot but of the ball only, with parts of the toes and the suggestion of claws.

"You found somethin'?" Wayland asked.

"Keep an eye on the woods, not me," Fargo said. Holding on to the Ovaro's reins, he covered a fair distance, finding partial tracks here and there to guide him.

They came to a hill. A broken plant showed where the Terror had borne to the west. A brown smear on a broad leaf showed something else. Breaking the leaf off, Fargo held it to the sunlight to be sure.

"What do you have there?" General Canton said.

"Dried blood."

"Then we did hit it," Hosiah said. "I knew I couldn't have missed, not that close I couldn't."

Fargo let the leaf fall and moved on. He was impressed by how little sign the creature left. And the farther they went, the harder it became to find.

By noon they were sweltering in the heat. They stopped briefly at a brackish ribbon of a creek to let the horses drink.

Not half an hour later they came to a steep embankment and climbed to the crest.

"Oh, hell," Hosiah said.

Ahead stretched unbroken swamp, a morass of pools and bogs bisected by channels of still water. Here and there were islands overgrown with near-impenetrable tangles of rank growth. Tall trees laden with vines and coated with moss stood in perpetual shadow. An unnatural stillness prevailed, and a quiet that gave no hint of the legion of snakes and alligators that lurked in the vegetation or the watery depths.

"We need a canoe or a boat," Wayland said.

"Neither of which we have," General Canton said.

"We sure can't take our horses in there," Hosiah said. "We're askin' for grief if'n we do."

Fargo swung down. Their quarry had descended a short slope and waded into a pool. He was about to wade out, too, when he spied bulges: the eyes and snout of a gator.

"We might have no recourse but to go around," General Canton said.

"There's no tellin' how far this swamp goes," Wayland said. "It could take days, if not longer."

"What else, then?" Canton said.

Fargo scratched his chin and pondered their dilemma. They were beaten unless he could come up with something. He considered using logs with branches for paddles. It would be slow going and they'd have to leave someone with their horses but they could keep after the Terror.

Then he gazed to the northwest.

"Do you gents see what I see?"

22

"Smoke, by heaven!" General Canton exclaimed.

"Don't get your hopes up," Wayland said. "It could be swamp rats or Injuns, for all we know."

"Do you always look at the bright side?" Fargo said. Climbing up the bank, he pointed at a log he'd noticed earlier. "Two of us will take that and have a look-see."

"Why not just swim while you're at it," Wayland said sarcastically. "You'll have as much chance of gettin' there alive."

"It's only a quarter of a mile," was Fargo's guess. "We can pole there in under an hour."

"Providin' a gator doesn't eat you or you get snakebit." Wayland shook his head. "Count me out. My ma didn't raise no stupids."

"I'll go," General Canton volunteered.

"It has to be me," Hosiah said.

"Why you?" Wayland demanded.

"Yes, why you?" Canton said.

"When was the last time you shot somethin'?" Hosiah asked. "Or even gone huntin'?"

The question seemed to bother the general. "I admit I haven't hunted in years. I've been working behind a desk." He frowned. "I see your point. I'm out of practice at this sort of thing." He looked at Fargo. "I'll leave it to you."

"Hosiah goes."

"I don't like us bein' separated, brother," Wayland said.

"I'll be all right," Hosiah said. "You just make damn sure these horses are here when we get back."

The log was newly fallen and heavy but the four of them easily rolled it down to the water and pushed it into the pool. Wayland made sure it wouldn't float off while Fargo and Hosiah sought suitable branches to trim for poles.

Before Fargo waded out to straddle the log, he cut a length of rope and tied one end to the Henry's barrel and the other end to the stock so he could sling the rifle across his back and free his hands for poling.

Hosiah did the same with his rifle.

To reduce the risk of being gator-bit, Fargo tucked his legs tight to the log and bent them back so his feet were out of the water.

Hosiah, again, did the same.

The pool fed into a narrow channel flanked by thick growth. Creepers hung so low that Fargo was constantly ducking. Now and then he glimpsed slithery shapes and once a small alligator rose up practically under the log and instantly flicked its tail and dived.

"Truth to tell," Hosiah remarked at that juncture, "I've never been all that fond of swamps."

"A man after my own heart," Fargo said.

"The way I see it, swamps are what the Good Lord had left over after He made everythin' else."

Fargo chuckled.

"All these bugs, the serpents, the gators," Hosiah said. "A swamp is a death trap waitin' to happen."

"Don't forget the Night Terror."

"Not hardly," Hosiah said.

They poled in silence after that. The channel wound into a cypress grove, which was good and bad. Good because they weren't hemmed by snake-infested growth. Bad because they had to wind among the boles, which slowed them considerably.

They were gliding through the last of the cypress when Fargo caught a whiff of a foul odor and quickly raised his pole and thrust it against a tree to bring the log to a stop.

"What is it?" Hosiah whispered.

"Bog," Fargo said, and pointed.

It was what the locals called any stretch of swamp that was more mud than water. While not as treacherous as quicksand, mud bogs could suck a person under if they weren't careful. And poling a log through one was next to impossible.

"Damn," Hosiah said.

They skirted it until they reached another channel. The detour cost them half an hour but eventually they neared a hummock fringed with chickweed and abundant with oaks and willows. The smoke rose from deeper in.

Fargo angled for an inlet in the shadow of overhanging willow branches. The log bumped shore and he slid off and held the log steady for Hosiah. Together they pulled the log high enough that it wouldn't drift off.

"Awful quiet," Hosiah whispered.

That it was. Birds should be singing but weren't. Nor did Fargo see the tracks of deer or other animals that usually came to the water to drink. Almost as if the wildlife shunned the place.

Unslinging the Henry, Fargo glided to a willow and crouched. A flickering orange finger confirmed there was a campfire. Motioning to Hosiah, he stalked from tree to tree.

A clearing opened. That, Fargo expected. He didn't expect to see a solitary figure hunkered despondently by the fire, her forearms on her knees, her chin on an arm.

"Eldrida Petrie!" Hosiah whispered.

Fargo could see that for himself. What he didn't see was the Night Terror. Flattening, he crawled to an oak a pebble's toss from the fire and lay perfectly still, waiting for some sign of her abductor.

Presently Eldrida stirred and sat up and gazed about her. She had a bruise on her cheek and a hen's egg on her forehead.

Fargo took a gamble. Rising on an elbow, he waved his other arm to draw her attention.

Eldrida saw him. She froze, then started to stand and opened her mouth as if to say something. Suddenly she stared fixedly at a thicket across the clearing, abruptly sat back down, and shook her head.

The Night Terror must be nearby. Fargo would have liked to spirit her out of there but the thing might have been watching.

"What are we waitin' for?" Hosiah whispered. "Let's get that poor gal and skedaddle."

"Not yet," Fargo said.

"We might not have another chance like this."

"No, damn it."

"Stay put if you want," Hosiah said, and took a half step around the oak he was behind.

Eldrida stiffened and frantically gestured for him to stop. She pointed at the thicket and silently mouthed a few words.

"What's she sayin'?" Hosiah whispered.

"I don't—" Fargo said, and got no further.

The thicket began to shake. Not part of it but the whole thing. A dark shadow at its center was unfolding and expanding into something huge and ominous.

"The Night Terror!" Hosiah hissed.

"Get down!"

Hosiah started to duck behind the tree, and froze, struck rigid by the sight of the thing that was emerging from the thicket.

Fargo's own blood turned to ice. He'd seen a lot of fearsome creatures in his travels, from ravening grizzlies and savage wolverines to rabid wolves. But he'd never, ever, seen anything like this.

23

The thing was huge, but they already knew that. In the light of day they saw *how* huge—over seven feet tall, closer to eight, with shoulders so broad it could never fit through a doorway unless it turned sideways.

The Terror wore what Fargo at first took to be a bearskin robe but was in fact a crudely fashioned poncho from a hide that had lost a lot of hair and was ripped in spots. The hide had a flap or hood that was pulled up over the Terror's head.

All Fargo could see of its face was a wide, misshapen nose. He thought of it as a "thing" even though it walked on two feet. They were misshapen, too, stumps of flesh with stubby toes capped by inches-long curved nails.

"Dear God," Hosiah Wilkes breathed.

The Terror reached the fire and pulled the hood down, and Fargo felt his skin crawl.

The thing's head was a travesty of how a head should be. Covered with bony bumps and knobs, the flesh lumpy and obscene, its features were twisted out of all proportion. One eye was higher than the other. A lipless mouth curled in a perpetual sneer. The teeth were all different sizes. One cheek bulged, the other was sunken. There was no chin, and there wasn't so much as a hair anywhere.

It reared over Eldrida Petrie and fixed eyes on her that didn't blink.

Fargo could tell she was afraid. Yet she met its stare and said, "Have you finally made up your mind to dispose of me?"

The thing uttered a strangled series of grunts and gurgles. It seemed to be trying to talk and gestured with hands twice the size of Fargo's, and as misshapen as the rest.

"I can't understand you, Cain," Eldrida said. "I try but I can't."

"Did she just call that thing by name?" Hosiah whispered.

Fargo was trying to make sense of it all when the creature called Cain removed the bear hide and let it drop to the ground.

Cain's body, like his head, was an abomination of how a body should be. Not just in size but because everything, every part and particle, was as deformed as the head and the feet. One shoulder curved up, the other down. One arm was longer, the shorter arm was thicker. Cain's enormous chest bulged and had bony bumps everywhere. Protuberances covered the stomach. The hips, in contrast to the chest, were narrow, while the legs were tree trunks with skin a lot like bark.

Fargo was dumbfounded. Never, even in the most rabid imaginings of a raving madman, had such a creature been conceived.

"What did you take that off for?" Eldrida demanded. "I don't care to see you naked. Put the hide back on."

Cain extended his long arm and his splayed fingers curled.

"I'm sorry for what they did to you," Eldrida said. "I don't suppose it helps much, but they thought you were dead."

Cain gurgled.

"How could they possibly guess you'd survive? No normal child would."

"What does all that mean?" Hosiah whispered.

Fargo didn't answer but a dark thought had taken root.

"I was born after they did it," Eldrida was saying. "I didn't hear about it until I was ten, I believe it was. Mother told me one night after she'd been drinking too much and I asked her why she and Father were always fighting. It was over you. Over what Father did."

Cain stood motionless, drool oozing over his lower lip.

"The horrors you must have gone through," Eldrida said. "The nightmares you must have endured."

Cain acted fascinated by her voice. He tilted his head and turned a deformed ear to her.

"I'm sincere when I say I'm sorry. No one should have to endure what you did."

With an angry movement, Cain suddenly grabbed the bear hide and pulled it over his head and shoulders.

"You're mad and I don't blame you," Eldrida said. "But what you're doing is wrong."

Cain uttered an angry snort.

"You can't go around killing folks. You can't take out your fury on people who had nothing to do with it."

Cain growled.

"All right," Eldrida said. "I won't talk about it if you don't want me to. Except to repeat that it's wrong to blame people who didn't even know you existed until you started ripping heads off. And to what end? How many more will you kill? You can't slay everybody, as much as you might like to."

Cain balled a gigantic fist.

"Go ahead. Hit me," Eldrida said. "It's the only way you'll keep me from saying my piece." She sadly bowed her head. "I should have told everyone who you are once I'd figured it out. They wouldn't be as scared, knowing you're a man. They'd hunt you down and finish what Ma and Pa started."

Unnoticed by Eldrida, Cain extended his other hand—reaching for her throat.

24

Fargo raised his Henry.

The creature called Cain suddenly lowered its hand and took a step back. He made sounds that might be speech. Then, wheeling, he placed his walnut-sized knuckles on the ground and lumbered off into the woods.

Eldrida called out, "Wait! Please! Won't you take me back? I don't want to be here."

Cain didn't look back.

The instant the giant was out of sight, Hosiah dashed toward the campfire.

"Damn it," Fargo said, and followed. He would have liked to wait a few minutes to be sure Cain was gone.

"Miss Petrie," Hosiah said. "You're safe now. We've come to rescue you."

Eldrida shot to her feet. "You fools," she exclaimed, glancing anxiously at where the abomination had vanished. "You'll get yourselves killed."

"Nice to see you, too," Fargo said.

Hosiah went to grasp Eldrida's arm but she jerked her hand away.

"Get out of here before it's too late. You were rash to come after me, and I won't have your deaths on my conscience."

"Quit your silliness," Hosiah said. "We're here to rescue you."

"Silly, am I?" Eldrida said.

"Silly as hell," Fargo told her.

"We're wastin' time." Hosiah grabbed her arm anyway. "Now let's light a shuck." He pulled but she dug in her heels. "What in tarnation is the matter with you? Not a minute ago I heard you tell that critter you wanted to go home."

"He's not a critter," Eldrida said. "He's a Petrie, the same as me."

"Tell us about him later," Fargo said, "and move your ass."

"I'll be damned if I will. You don't know what this is about. You don't know what harm you can do."

Fargo lost his temper. "You want harm?" he said, and before either of them could guess his intent, he stepped up and clubbed her with the Henry, a short, powerful stroke that felled her where she stood.

Hosiah caught Eldrida before she hit the ground and looked at Fargo in amazement. "What's gotten into you? You could have busted her skull."

"Not as thick as her head is." Fargo gripped Eldrida's other arm, hoisted her up, and nodded at the trees. "Get going before that thing comes back."

Hosiah didn't need urging. He fell into step, saying, "She'll be mad as hell when she comes around."

"Better mad than dead."

"I couldn't do what you just did. Our ma raised us to always be polite to womenfolk. A lady should be treated like a lady, she'd always say, even when they weren't."

"Hosiah," Fargo said.

"What?"

Fargo looked at him.

"Oh. I reckon now's not the time, huh?"

They hurried as best they could. Eldrida didn't weigh much over a hundred pounds but there was a lot of growth to push through. They reached the inlet and the water's edge.

"What do we do now?" Hosiah asked. "She'll fall off the log unless she's awake to hold on."

From the vicinity of the clearing came a loud crash.

"Cain," Hosiah whispered.

"Hold her," Fargo said. Setting the Henry down, he slid the log parallel to shore, then took Eldrida from Hosiah so Hosiah could straddle the log. Swinging Eldrida up and over, he leaned Eldrida against Hosiah's back.

"What are you doin'?"

"Your belt," Fargo said, "and the rope to your rifle sling."

"My britches will fall down."

Fargo snapped his fingers.

"I hope this works," Hosiah said as he complied.

Working quickly, Fargo tied the rope and belt together and passed them around Eldrida's waist and then around Hosiah's, and knotted them. "That will have to do. If you feel her sliding off, reach back and grab her."

"But my rifle," Hosiah said. "I won't have my hands free to pole."

"Leave the poling to me." Wading out, Fargo slung the Henry across his back and exercised care in taking his place on the log. A kick carried them clear. It was a lot harder with just one poling but he managed to turn the log and head back the way they came.

"She's sort of pretty, ain't she?" Hosiah had twisted his head and was admiring their unwilling passenger.

"Shouldn't you be watching for Cain?"

"Sorry." Hosiah tore his gaze from her. "It just makes me feel warm all over, this gal pressin' on me like she is."

"She's unconscious."

"I can still feel 'em."

Fargo didn't have to ask what the "'em" were.

"I only ever touched a pair once," Hosiah gabbed on. "They belonged to my cousin. She's pretty free with hers. But most girls hereabouts, if'n you touch them when they don't want you to, they're liable to cut your pecker off. I'm fond of mine."

"Hosiah."

"What?"

"You're doing it again."

They made slow progress. Skirting the mud bog seemed to take hours. Any moment, Fargo expected to hear the crash of undergrowth.

Hosiah must have been thinking the same thing because at one point he said, "Strange that the critter hasn't come after us."

"Maybe he's wary of our guns."

"I doubt that critter is afraid of anything this side of hell," Hosiah said. "Which, come to think of it, could be where it's from."

Out of nowhere Eldrida said, "He was born of woman, the same as you and me. I'll thank you to remember that."

"You've come around!" Hosiah happily declared. "I was worried you were bad hurt."

"I have a headache but otherwise I appear to be fine. No thanks to *him*."

Fargo kept on poling.

"Why am I trussed to you, Mr. Wilkes?" Eldrida asked Hosiah. "It's unseemly for us to touch in this manner."

"We didn't want you fallin' off," Hosiah said.

"I demand you untie me."

"Sure," Hosiah replied.

"No," Fargo said.

"No?" From Eldrida.

"You'll stay put until we get to our horses. Then we're taking you to the hunting lodge."

"Who do you think you are? I'll raise a fuss, by God, and he'll hear it."

"I knocked you out once," Fargo said. "I can do it again."

Eldrida was quiet a bit, then said, "You're not very nice."

"And you're turning into a bitch."

Hosiah interrupted their dispute with, "I want to hear about the critter, Miss Petrie. What can you tell us?"

"Stop calling him that," Eldrida said. "He's a person like you and me."

"He didn't look like any person I ever saw," Hosiah said. "What was that business about it bein' born of a woman, anyhow?"

Eldrida sighed. "Very well. I suppose you have a right to know if anyone does. Here are the facts."

25

Fargo listened with half an ear while poling and staying alert for signs of pursuit. That Cain hadn't given chase was both a relief and a puzzlement.

"I suspected who the Night Terror was when I heard a description of the killer," Eldrida Petrie commenced her account. "I remembered the child's great size was one of the things that frightened everyone so much."

"Hold up there, pretty gal," Hosiah said. "What child?"

"Sorry." Eldrida coughed. "Aaron, my older brother, isn't really the oldest. Ten years before he was born, my mother had her first child, and the poor infant was a scandal from the day she gave birth."

"Why a scandal?" Hosiah asked.

"Because she had him less than six months after she said her vows. You see, she was in the family way before she was wed. My father married her because she was pregnant, and because it was the right thing to do."

"Noble of him," Fargo said.

Eldrida paid him no mind. "Her parents hushed it up. You can imagine the gossip that would have spread had word gotten out. Their plan was to keep the baby a secret until nine months had gone by, and then let it be known she'd given birth."

"Who cares what folks would have said?" Hosiah said. "In our family, babies are born out of wedlock all the time."

"Not in my family. To my grandparents, their social standing was everything. They were well-to-do. Pillars of the community. They attended church every week, and Grandfather was a deacon. They wouldn't hear of their son having a bastard child, if you'll pardon my language."

"I'd pardon anything you wanted me to," Hosiah said.

Fargo smothered a snort.

"The wedlock situation was only part of it," Eldrida said. "The worst part was that the baby came out . . . deformed."

"You're not sayin' that thing back there—?"

"Is Cain, my mother's firstborn. The baby was so hideous, a midwife ran from the room screaming."

"I don't blame her," Hosiah said. "I want to scream myself when I set eyes on that crit—uh—thing."

"The baby revolted my father," Eldrida said. "He believed the baby couldn't possibly be his. That Mother had slept with another man, and the baby bore the mark of Cain as punishment for their sin."

"You mean the Cain from the Bible?" Hosiah said.

"The very one. Father wanted nothing to do with the baby but Mother wouldn't hear of that. She insisted they keep Cain, and they did for five years or so. Then one day she went off to New Orleans and left Cain with the nanny. When she came home, he was gone."

"Where to?" Hosiah asked.

"It was Father's doing. He couldn't take the sight of the boy anymore. So he had some men row Cain out into the swamp and leave him there."

"Noble as hell," Fargo said.

"You weren't there," Eldrida snapped. "I agree it's terrible but Father had the welfare of the family to think about. He used to say that the Spartans did the same thing with their deformed babies."

"The who?" Hosiah said.

"My point is," Eldrida said, "that my father expected the baby would die and put an end to their shame. Somehow, though, Cain survived. Can you imagine what it must have been like for him? All alone in the middle of that terrible swamp? What did he eat? How did he get by? That an alligator never ate him or he wasn't snakebit or got sucked into quicksand is a miracle."

"He might not have seen other people for a long time," Hosiah remarked.

"That could well be. Maybe one day he did, and followed them out of the swamp. Or else he wandered out on his own. And that's when the killing began."

"Why kill folks?" Hosiah said. "You'd think he'd be happy to be around other people again."

"Revenge," Fargo said.

"That would be my guess," Eldrida surprised him by agreeing. "Cain remembers being abandoned and hates what was done to him."

"So he rips the heads off everybody?" Hosiah said.

"You have to remember," Eldrida said. "He's still a little boy stuck in that horrid body."

"Little boys don't rip off heads," Hosiah said.

"Beasts do," Fargo said.

"What are you saying?" Eldrida asked.

"All those years in the wilds have turned him wild," Fargo speculated. "He's more animal than boy."

"If that's the case, why didn't he kill me?"

"Or you for that matter. Why didn't he kill you that day you found our cousin's head?" Hosiah said.

Fargo didn't have an answer.

"I tried to reason with him," Eldrida said. "Once I got over my fear and realized he wasn't going to hurt me."

"Maybe he wanted you for something else," Fargo suggested.

"What would that be?" Eldrida said, and then, emphatically, "No. Absolutely not. He never laid a finger on me. Not that way. To think he would is despicable."

"He's not a boy anymore."

"Who can say if he even feels the urge?" Hosiah said. "A body like he has isn't normal like ours."

"That part would be."

"He didn't touch me, I tell you," Eldrida said. "Besides, I'm his sister."

"He doesn't know that."

"Perhaps he does. Perhaps that's why he didn't harm me."

"We'll find out soon enough how he feels," Fargo said.

"How so?" Hosiah asked.

Fargo pointed behind them. "Because here he comes."

26

A quarter of a mile back, a gargantuan figure barreled after them like a rampaging bull. Nothing stood in its way. Brush, thickets, reeds, were plowed through as if they didn't exist. Even saplings were flattened with an ease that was frightening. Water was no obstacle whatsoever. The living dreadnought surged through it as a ship would, leaving a wide wake.

"God Almighty," Hosiah exclaimed.

"Nothing stops him," Eldrida said. "Not nothing at all."

Fargo believed her. He could imagine snakes and gators stampeded by the sudden noise and fury. He gazed ahead, calculating how far they had to go to reach the horses. "We'll never make it."

"That critter catches us, it'll rip us to bits," Hosiah said.

"I told you to stop calling him that. He has a name. Cain Petrie," Eldrida said.

"You can call him whatever you like, pretty lady," Hosiah said. "To me he's a critter and nothin' more."

"How about you?" Eldrida said to Fargo. "Do you think of him as a monster, too?"

"Hell, no. He's a regular daisy."

Hosiah laughed.

"Men and their humor," Eldrida said.

They neared an island, no more than an eighth of an acre sprinkled with a few oaks.

"There," Fargo said, and poled toward it.

"What are you doing?" Eldrida asked.

"We're making a stand," Fargo informed her. They didn't stand a prayer on the log. One sweep of Cain's arm and they'd be upended.

"How do we stop it?" Hosiah said. "Bullets didn't do much the last time."

"We'll shoot smarter," Fargo said.

"How in blazes do we do that?"

"Hold on." Fargo jabbed the pole at a floating log to avoid a collision, and once around it, navigated past a spur of land to a flat belt of shore. He untied Eldrida and she glared the whole time.

89

"I don't want him hurt, you hear me?" she said as Fargo helped her off the log. "He's not to blame for what he does. He's not in his right mind."

"He tries to rip off my head," Fargo said, "he's dead."

"Same here," Hosiah said. "I'm sorry, pretty lady. The Good Book says to turn the other cheek but I don't have a second head to turn."

"Please," Eldrida said. "He's misguided, is all."

"He's loco," Fargo said, "and so are you." All those years alone in the swamp had done something to the boy's mind. Made it more beast than human. Or maybe Cain Petrie had been that way from birth. Maybe that was another reason the father banished his son to the wilds. Maybe it wasn't just the body that was deformed. Maybe the boy's mind had been deformed, too.

Hosiah helped him pull the log out of the water. Rifles in hand, they moved to where they could see the juggernaut bearing down on them. Cain was still a ways off but they heard the tremendous racket he raised.

"Look at him," Hosiah said in awe. "I'd quake in my boots if it wouldn't be embarrassin'."

"All I feel for him is pity," Eldrida said. "He's a sweet child trapped in that terrible body. Rejected by those he loved. Banished from human company. Anyone would act as he does."

"All I know," Hosiah said, "is that I'm not hankerin' to die."

"Makes two of us," Fargo said, and jacked the lever to feed a cartridge into the Henry.

"Try to scare him off," Eldrida said. "Don't shoot to kill unless you absolutely have to."

"Scare *that* off?" Hosiah said. "I could have a cannon pointed at that thing and I doubt it'd be afraid."

"You have to try something," Eldrida insisted.

"We could sing to it," Fargo said, "but I left my piano in Denver." Hosiah chuckled.

"You're not half as funny as you think you are," Eldrida said. "If you won't try, I will."

"What can you do?" Hosiah asked.

Cain had reached the last channel of water. Huffing and puffing, he churned his thick legs like pistons. He spied them and jerked his head up and slowed.

"Uh-oh," Hosiah said.

Eldrida smiled and waved. "Cain!" she hollered. "It's me! Remember? The one who's been nice to you."

Cain lumbered to a stop. He was in rifle range but it would be a long shot and Fargo wanted to be sure when he squeezed the trigger.

"It's Eldrida," Eldrida shouted. "Your sister. You spared me. You were kind to me, remember?" She waved some more.

Cain raised a misshapen hand and imitated her.

"See?" Eldrida said excitedly. "He understands."

"You can't trust him," Fargo warned.

"But don't you see? That's partly why he's so bitter. No one has ever shown they cared enough to trust him."

"You're assumin' it thinks like us and maybe it doesn't," Hosiah echoed Fargo's worry.

"I have to try, I tell you." Eldrida took several steps and spread her arms. "I won't hurt you, Cain. I'll never hurt you. I'm the one true friend you have in this world."

"I don't like this," Hosiah whispered.

"Be ready," Fargo whispered back.

Cain Petrie waded closer, moving slowly, his face twisted as if in confusion.

"I'm your sister," Eldrida said, her voice quavering with emotion. "We're kin. You can trust me, Cain." She took a few more steps.

"That's far enough," Fargo said.

Cain stopped. He tossed his head back and forth, then pressed a hand to his brow.

"What's he doin'?" Hosiah wondered.

"How the hell would I know?" Fargo said.

Eldrida took another step. "Do you understand, Cain? Am I getting through to you? We're not your enemies. We're friends."

"I think she's doin' it, by God," Hosiah said.

Cain had lowered his hand and did appear to be trying to smile. He spread his huge arms wider and advanced, his mismatched eyes gleaming with what might be affection.

"He's like a great big dog," Hosiah said.

Fargo still wasn't convinced. He wedged the Henry to his shoulder and fixed a bead on the monstrosity's head.

"Yes, Cain, yes," Eldrida was saying. "We're friends. Be nice to us and we'll be nice to you. Isn't that what you want? For people to like you? For people to show they care?"

Cain reached the island. He was still smiling, his arms still spread wide.

"This is it," Hosiah said.

"Come to me, Cain," Eldrida said. "Come hug the sister you never knew you had."

27

Fargo curled his finger to the trigger. He would shoot at the first hint of danger to Eldrida.

"Oh, Cain," she gushed, beside herself with joy. "You make me so happy. I knew I could get through to you. I just knew it."

Cain Petrie towered over her like a redwood over a rose. His lipless mouth twitched and what appeared to be tears were trickling down his face.

"Will you look at that," Hosiah Wilkes marveled.

"I can help you, Cain," Eldrida said enthusiastically. "I can teach you things. You can come live at the lodge and learn to be human again."

"The law won't go for that," Hosiah said so only Fargo heard. "She's forgettin' all the folks he's killed."

The giant's likely fate, Fargo mused, would be life in prison or a strangulation jig at the end of a rope.

Eldrida put her hand to Cain's chest. "I'm sorry for what our father did to you. I'm sorry for the years you've spent by your lonesome in the swamp. That's over now. I'll take care of you. I'll help you every way I can."

Cain was motionless except for his twitching lip.

"At first I thought you were nothing but a brute. But when you took me and didn't hurt me, I saw the truth. Deep down you're still a little boy. You really don't want to hurt people. You've only done it because they hurt you. Because Father cast you aside as if you were worthless."

"She should stop," Hosiah said.

Cain bent toward Eldrida, his twisted smile widening.

"Yes, yes," she said warmly. "I'm your sister and your friend and you can trust me forever."

Cain began to lower his arms.

"I can make up for the injustice done you. You'll have a whole new life." Eldrida placed her hand on his chest and craned her neck back to look him in the face. "You can start over. I'll convince them that punishing you would be wrong. You can't be held to account when you didn't know any better."

Cain grunted.

"I'll persuade them to let me watch over you. You'll be fed, sheltered, have a roof over your head."

Cain uttered a soft sound, like the coo of a dove, and gently placed his knobby hands on Eldrida's slim shoulders. He closed his mismatched eyes and shuddered.

"What's he doin'?" Hosiah said.

Fargo almost shouted to Eldrida not to let Cain touch her but his yell might provoke Cain into attacking. Quietly, he said, "Eldrida, you should back away."

Eldrida glanced over at them. Tears glistened, and she had to cough to say, "Don't be ridiculous. Can't you see I've tamed him? He wouldn't harm a fly now. Lower your guns. There's no need for them."

"You shouldn't ought to let him touch you," Hosiah cautioned.

Eldrida looked up at Cain. "I'm so happy right now. Mother would be, too, were she alive. You've come back into the fold."

Cain cooed, and in a blur his hands were around her throat. His shoulders bunched and his arms rippled, and with an incredibly powerful wrench he tore Eldrida Petrie's head from her body. Scarlet sprayed in a fountain and her body began to crumble.

Eldrida had no time to cry out, no chance to resist. One moment she was smiling, the next blood spurted from her mouth.

Fargo had never seen anyone move as fast as Cain. Belatedly, he stroked the trigger and the Henry boomed and bucked.

By rights Cain should have died then and there. But the lead intended for his head struck Eldrida's as he raised hers into the air.

Hosiah fired, too, yelling, "You killed her, you bastard!"

His fingers entwined in Eldrida's hair, Cain whirled and plunged into the swamp.

Fargo aimed at the back of the creature's head but as he went to shoot, Cain dived.

"Damn it all!" Hosiah cried, reloading as he rushed to the water's edge.

Fargo fired four shots as rapidly as he could at the spot where Cain had gone under. Hopeful, he scanned the surface for signs of blood or bubbles.

"One of us had to have hit it," Hosiah said.

Twenty yards out a few ripples appeared.

"Him, you reckon?" Hosiah said.

Fargo trained his Henry but nothing else happened. Long minutes dragged until finally he lowered the rifle and admitted, "He got away."

"Underwater?"

"How else?" Fargo rejoined. It made sense that Cain had learned to swim. Swamps were mostly water, after all.

"What now? Do we wait around for it to come after us again?"

"We do not." Fargo turned to the body. A red pool had formed with more blood seeping from the stump.

"Should we bury her?" Hosiah asked.

"No."

"That's harsh. She was a sweet gal."

"Her sweetness got her killed." Fargo stepped to the log, slung his Henry, and pushed. "If you're coming, hop on."

"You don't leave a fella much choice," Hosiah complained.

"You're welcome to stay and add your head to Cain's collection."

"I reckon I'll pass on that."

Acutely conscious of the dark water around and under them, and what might be lurking in it, Fargo used the pole to keep his balance. "Hurry up."

"I'm comin'. I'm comin'." Hosiah moved to the other end and slid on, freezing when the log shifted and almost rolled. "There," he said as it settled. "You want me to cover you like before?"

"You read my mind."

An eternity of poling ensued. Fargo's shoulder grew sore, his arms weary, but he would be damned if he'd stop. They never knew when Cain might erupt out of the water or come crashing through the brush.

Hosiah was unusually quiet. Not until they came in sight of the embankment did he venture to say, "I've changed my mind about avengin' Jerrod. Goin' after that critter in its own element would be plumb foolish."

"Your brothers might not agree."

"Abimelech will do whatever I say. Wayland might raise a fuss but he won't go after the thing without us." Hosiah raised a hand to shield his eyes from the sun. "Say, where's Thaddeus and him, anyhow? Shouldn't they be waitin' for us?"

There was no sign of either.

"Maybe they're lying low," Fargo said.

"When they can see us comin' as plain as can be?" Hosiah suddenly straightened. "Say, is that a body?"

28

Sprawled half over the bank and barely visible in the high grass was a human figure. A hat lay nearby, upside down, and the stock of a rifle poked out.

"That's Wayland!" Hosiah exclaimed. "Pole faster."

Fargo jammed the pole against the bottom and levered it. He reasoned that if Wayland was down, General Canton must be too, and he had a good idea who the culprits were. He mentally swore at himself for leaving Canton behind, but what else could he do?

"Wayland!" Hosiah hollered. "Can you hear me?"

"Canton!" Fargo called out.

They were in chest-high water when Hosiah slid off the log and frantically made for shore. He didn't care that he got water on his rifle. Heaving onto land, he scrambled up the bank, saying Wayland's name over and over.

The log bumped and Fargo vaulted off. He reached Wayland only a couple of steps behind Hosiah, who grabbed his brother and rolled him over with his head in his lap.

"Wayland? Speak to me."

Wayland groaned.

"He's alive!" Hosiah slid his hand under his brother's back and recoiled and slid it out again. His palm was smeared red. "Blood!"

With Fargo helping, they eased Wayland onto his side and examined him. Hosiah touched a red-rimmed slit in his brother's shirt between Wayland's shoulder blades and his face went white.

"He's been stabbed."

"Get his shirt off while I look for Canton."

The general was nowhere to be found. Nor was his mount. Fargo did find the tracks of two horses that had arrived while he and Hosiah were off in the swamp and then gone off again with the general's horse between them. He was pondering the implications when Hosiah called out.

"Help me, will you? We need to clean his wound and bandage him."

Fargo kindled a fire and put water on to boil while Hosiah spread out a bedroll and placed his brother on a blanket, belly-down.

"Whoever did this missed his heart," Hosiah said grimly. "It's the only reason he's still alive."

Fargo thought he knew who might be to blame. If he was right, then Canton didn't have long to live. In fact, it surprised him that they hadn't stabbed the general, too, and taken what they were after. He wanted to give chase but he couldn't bring himself to desert Hosiah, not when Cain Petrie might be lurking nearby.

"Who could have done this?" Hosiah asked. "And where the hell is Thaddeus Canton?"

Fargo told him about the two riders.

"And you say he went with them? What for? And why did they try to kill my brother?"

"We'll find out when we catch up to them," Fargo hedged.

When the water was hot, Hosiah cleaned and dressed Wayland's wound. He discovered that the blade had gone in at an angle and likely missed the heart by an inch or less.

As Hosiah was putting his brother's shirt back on, Wayland stirred and his eyelids fluttered.

"What—?" he said thickly.

"You've done been knifed," Hosiah said quickly. "Don't try to talk. Just lie here and rest."

Wayland licked his lips and swallowed. "Who?"

"Don't know yet," Hosiah said. "I thought maybe Thaddeus, although why in hell he'd stab you is beyond me. But Fargo found where a couple of riders showed up. Who were they?"

"Never heard or saw no riders," Wayland said.

"That's not important right now. Rest easy and we'll head out in the mornin' if you're up to it."

"We can't spend the night here," Fargo said, and gestured at the swamp.

Hosiah frowned. "Wayland shouldn't be moved. Not this soon."

"What's he talkin' about?" Wayland asked. "And where's the Petrie lady? Why ain't she with you?"

Fargo let Hosiah explain while he watched for Cain. Once he glimpsed something off in a cluster of cypress but it could have been an animal.

Wayland voiced his disgust when his brother finished by saying, "So Papa Petrie had his kid dumped in the swamp and left him there because he was born ugly? I always knew they were too high-and-mighty for their own good."

"You haven't seen it. I can't say as I blame him," Hosiah said.

Wayland gazed skyward. "It'll be dark in a couple of hours. If that thing is out there, we should skedaddle while we have daylight left."

"We're stayin' until you're fit to ride."

"I'm fit now."

"You were stabbed, you idiot," Hosiah said.

"But it don't hurt much and I didn't lose much blood," Wayland said. "Sittin' a saddle for a while won't kill me."

"I say no."

Wayland appealed to Fargo. "How about you, mister? What do you say?"

Fargo locked eyes with Hosiah. "You saw what Cain did to his sister. You saw how fast he is, and how hard he is to kill. Once it's dark he'll sneak in close and I wouldn't give a wooden nickel for our chances."

"I can ride, big brother," Wayland said. "And a knife wound ain't nothin' compared to havin' my head tore off."

Hosiah glumly stared at the foreboding quagmire below the embankment and came to the only decision he could. "We'll light a shuck."

29

Fargo kept expecting to find General Canton's body somewhere along the trail to the lodge. He was relieved that they didn't, but at the same time, it confounded him no end.

Wayland Wilkes held up well. He was hurting but he grit his teeth and never once complained. He did ask that they stop a couple of times so he could rest a bit.

Fargo was glad to. They'd put several miles between them and the swamp, and there was no sign that Cain Petrie was after them. Wishful thinking on his part, Fargo reckoned. But the farther away they were, the better the likelihood they had seen the last of him.

Fargo's main concern now was Canton, and the secret report he'd toted for hundreds of miles in the dispatch pouch. He hadn't gone to all that trouble to have it stolen by what the general liked to call "the other side."

About halfway to the hunting lodge, Hosiah brought his mount alongside the Ovaro. "We need to talk."

"Oh?"

"What in hell is goin' on? These tracks we've been followin' are leadin' us back to that lodge."

"So I've noticed."

"Why?"

Fargo was stumped there.

"I don't hear you talkin'."

"I don't know," Fargo admitted.

"You know somethin'," Hosiah said. "You and Thaddeus have been real secretive. About what?"

After all they'd been through, Fargo felt he owed him an explanation. But he'd given his word to keep the troop report secret. So he settled for "Army stuff."

"It has nothin' to do with the Night Terror?"

"Nothing at all."

"Does it involve those females?"

"It might."

"Could it be them as stabbed Wayland?"

"It could."

"And we left Abimelech with them." Hosiah swore, then said, "You couldn't have warned us they might be up to no good?"

"I wasn't sure."

"A poor excuse," Hosiah said. "I've got one brother stabbed, and who knows what they've done to the other one."

"I gave my word," Fargo said.

"To who? The army?"

"To keep what it's about a secret."

"Well, hell. I guess I can't hold it against you, then. A man's got to keep his word or he ain't much of a man."

"For what it's worth," Fargo said, "I'd tell you everything if it was up to me."

"That's worth a lot." Hosiah chewed his bottom lip. "Do you reckon they've killed Abimelech?"

"No reason for them to."

"I hope you're right. And just so you know, army or no army, those gals have to answer for Wayland."

"Do what you have to."

"You won't mind?"

"It could just as well have been me they stuck the blade into."

"I don't much cotton to hurtin' females but a knife in the back is as dirty as you can go."

The sun set and they pushed on. It was about ten, by Fargo's estimation, when they reached the forest flanking the hunting lodge. Ahead, through the trees, glowed a rectangle of light.

"They're there, by God," Hosiah said.

"Someone is," Fargo said.

They drew rein at the tree line and dismounted. Wayland had to be helped. He was so weak, he could barely hold his head up.

"Stay with him and I'll have a look-see," Fargo suggested.

"Abimelech is my brother. I should be the one." Hosiah stared at the glowing window. "But go get it done."

Palming his Colt, Fargo sprinted to the lodge. Keeping low, he edged under the window, removed his hat, and peered in.

It was the kitchen. A coffeepot was on the stove and several plates and cups on the table. Three people had eaten a meal earlier. Abimelech and the women, Fargo figured. Shoving his hat on, he worked his way around to the front.

A single horse was at the hitch rail.

Fargo edged to the door. They'd left it partway open. He gave a push and darted inside. The first thing he saw were legs sticking from behind the settee. The second thing he saw was the crimson sheen of dry blood.

Fargo went to the settee.

Abimelech lay on his back, an arm outflung, his other hand pressed to his throat to stanch the bleeding. Not that it would have done any good. Someone had slit him from ear to ear. His face mirrored his shock.

Fargo was sure no one else was there but he checked anyway. As he was coming up the hall he saw Hosiah and Wayland by the settee, the oldest supporting his brother, both transfixed with horror. He could think of nothing to say except, "I'm sorry for you."

Hosiah tore his gaze from the slit throat. "Was your word worth his life?"

No answer would do and Fargo didn't give any.

"We bury him in the mornin' and go after them," Wayland said.

"I'll see to the grave," Hosiah said. "As for goin' after them, that depends on how soon you mend."

"I'm able to, I tell you."

"Sure you are."

Fargo went outside. He was bone tired but his mind raced. Things didn't add up. Abimelech had to have been killed before Belinda and Adelade set out after Canton. Why did they bring the general back to the lodge? Why was Canton still breathing? All they had to do was kill him and take the documents.

He was mulling it over when the door opened and out came Hosiah.

"I finally got Wayland to sleep. He's powerful upset about his brother. They were close, those two. Even more than Abimelech and me."

"I can't stick around for the burial," Fargo informed him.

"Didn't reckon you would." Hosiah leaned against a post and sadly regarded the stars. "It's just as well. Wayland is in no shape for a hard ride. It'll be two or three days before he'll be fit enough."

"With any luck it'll be over by then."

"I won't ask you not to," Hosiah said. "Even though by rights it should be us who does them in." He paused. "Tell me somethin'. This friend of yours. Thaddeus. I never did know him that well. What's his part in all this?"

"He has something those women want."

"Why haven't they taken it and done away with him like they did Abimelech and tried to do with Wayland?"

"If I knew that," Fargo said, "I'd be a happy man."

30

Fargo wasn't asleep an hour when the Ovaro whinnied. He had stretched out on the floor with his bedroll for a pillow. Now, sitting up, he forced his sluggish brain to work. The stallion seldom nickered without cause.

Something was out there.

Rising, Fargo grabbed the Henry and cat-footed to the front door. Over by the hearth, Hosiah and Wayland both snored. Neither woke when he worked the latch and slipped out.

After the oppressive heat of the day, the cool of night was a relief. It was still muggy but bearable.

Fargo moved to the hitch rail.

All four horses were staring toward the high reeds, their nostrils flaring. They'd caught a scent they didn't like.

Fargo hoped it was a bear or a gator. He hunkered down to await developments.

The horses went on staring. Twice the reeds rustled but it could have been the breeze.

Fatigue returned. It became a struggle to stay alert. He'd about decided it was nothing to worry about when the reeds rustled louder than before and out lumbered a gigantic bulk on all fours.

The short hairs at the nape of Fargo's neck prickled. He slowly raised the Henry and sighted down the barrel but it was so dark, he couldn't see the front sight and had to aim by instinct.

Despite his bulk, Cain Petrie was a virtual wraith. He made no sound as he stalked forward.

Fargo couldn't guess his intent. Drive the horses off? Kill them? He eased back the hammer so the click wouldn't be loud but fifty feet out the gigantic figure stopped and crouched.

A growl rumbled from Cain's barrel chest.

Fargo fired, pumped the lever, fired a second time. At the first shot, Cain whirled and streaked like lightning for the reeds. At the second shot Cain seemed to stumble but it could have been Fargo's imagination.

The reeds closed around him.

Levering another round into the chamber, Fargo backed toward the front door. A cry inside told him the Wilkeses were awake, and Hosiah charged out with his rifle at the ready.

"What is it? Why did you shoot?"

"Cain Petrie," Fargo said.

"Did you hit him? Is he done for?"

"I doubt it."

Hosiah cursed luridly.

Wayland appeared, moving slowly, half bent over. "What's the ruckus?" he asked, and coughed.

"You shouldn't be out here," Hosiah said, wrapping an arm around him. "You need more rest."

"I won't be babied," Wayland said. "What was the shootin' about?"

"The Night Terror."

"If it ain't chickens, it's feathers," Wayland said. "But he doesn't scare me pea green anymore. Not knowin' he's human like you and me."

"He is and he ain't," Hosiah said.

"Maybe we've never seen his like, like you say," Wayland said, "but a bullet will kill him the same as it kills anybody."

Fargo let him think what he wanted.

Hosiah, though, said, "You listen to me, brother, and you listen good. This Cain Petrie ain't like nothin' we've ever come across. He'll send us to hell and gone unless we're mighty careful. Don't take him lightly."

"I don't care a whit if'n he's the Devil himself," Wayland said. "We owe him for Jerrod." He coughed and doubled over. "Reckon I'd better lie back down. Give a holler if'n you need me."

"I've got me a fine brother there," Hosiah said in admiration.

"I'm going in after him."

"Him who? Wayland or Petrie?"

Fargo moved around the rail.

"Are you addlepated?" Hosiah asked. "That critter will break you in half. Let's bar the door and fort up until daybreak."

"There are other ways in," Fargo said, "and we can't cover them all. By taking the fight to him, I'll keep him too busy to try to slip inside."

"He might outwit you. Let you stumble around out there while he does what you don't want him to."

"That's where you come in," Fargo said. "Protect your brother."

"If we had a ladder I'd climb on the roof," Hosiah said. "It's the only place we'd be halfway safe."

Fargo had wasted enough time. He crept forward. The breeze had died and the reeds were still.

"I wish you wouldn't," Hosiah tried a last time.

Fargo looked back and motioned for quiet. It would be hard enough to hear Cain over the chorus of frogs and gators.

The reeds were a mire of shadow. A bull buffalo could be standing in there and no one would know it.

Fargo's mouth went dry. At one time or another he'd stalked grizzlies, mountain lions, and Apaches. None worried him like Cain Petrie, a mountain of muscle wedded to pure bloodlust, and next to unstoppable.

Images of Eldrida filled his head and he shrugged them away.

Fargo came to the reeds. They grew so close together they were a virtual wall.

No matter where he entered them, their swaying would give him away.

Fargo girded himself. He had to do it. When he lit out after the general and the women in the morning, he didn't want to be looking over his shoulder every mile of the way.

As if he were molasses, Fargo stuck the Henry's muzzle between some reeds and parted them.

The stillness was unnerving. For a few moments he thought he heard heavy breathing. His skin crawled as he slipped through the gap he'd made and let the reeds close behind him. They hemmed him like so many bars. He couldn't see over them. He couldn't see into them.

He must rely on his ears and his nose more than his eyes.

A minute or more went by. He was sure he heard breathing, but from where? Straight ahead? To the right? The left?

Hosiah may have had a point. Maybe this was a mistake.

The feeble starlight was no help. Fargo couldn't see the Henry in his own hands.

But he did spy a glint as of faint light reflected off metal. He was trying to figure what it could be when the "glint" blinked.

It was Cain Petrie's eye.

31

For an instant Fargo was riveted with surprise. But only for an instant. He pointed the Henry and fired even as the reeds exploded and Cain Petrie hurtled at him like a living avalanche. He jacked the lever to fire again but Cain was on him before he could shoot.

It was akin to being slammed into by a battering ram. Fargo was swept off his feet and propelled out of the reeds as if shot from a cannon. He landed with jolting force on his back and barely had time to register Cain's bulk sweeping toward him when a foot caught him in the side. He flew head over boots, awash in agony, and crashed onto his side.

Fargo managed to sit up and swing toward the reeds. He raised the Henry and thumbed back the hammer.

Cain was coming at him again, that bear hide rendering him as black as the night. His hands were outstretched to grip and rend and his teeth were bared in his perpetual sneer.

Fargo aimed at Cain's head and fired.

With a howl of rage, Cain veered. Another shot from the direction of the hunting lodge caused Cain to spin and in three long bounds he was back in the reeds.

Fargo shakily rose. Behind him boots thumped and Hosiah Wilkes came running up.

"I thought he had you."

"Makes two of us," Fargo said. His ribs were on fire. It was a miracle they weren't staved in.

"I can't get over how fast that critter is," Hosiah said.

"You and me, both."

"Do we go in after it?"

"We do not." Fargo had learned his lesson. In the reeds, Cain had the advantage. "We let him come to us."

"Fine by me," Hosiah said. "I thought you were loco to do what you did. I wouldn't for anything."

They cautiously backed toward the lodge.

"Could be the critter will try for our horses," Hosiah speculated. "If'n it strands us here, we'll be no better off than Eldrida."

Which was why Fargo had made up his mind to keep their animals under guard. "We'll take turns keeping watch. I'll take the first watch. Get what sleep you can. At dawn we'll head out."

"If that critter will let us."

"I hope it tries," Fargo said grimly. In daylight he could put a slug in its brainpan and end this.

"It'd please me no end if it just went off into the swamps, where it belongs."

"What about Jerrod?"

"Avengin' him is provin' harder than I thought. And I want whoever killed Abimelech more. Whichever of those gals is to blame has to answer for it."

Fargo stopped at the hitch rail. "Keep the fire burning. You'll need the light if he gets past me."

"Hell, for two bits I'd set those reeds on fire. But this time of year, the whole countryside would go up." Hosiah went in.

Fargo moved to a shadowed spot so he'd be harder to see. He leaned his back to the wall and gingerly touched his side and winced. He wished he had some whiskey. It would help with the pain.

The shots had silenced the wildlife but now the thrum of insects and the croak of frogs resumed.

Fargo heard only a few gators. There weren't many near the lodge, thank God.

Cain Petrie was enough to worry about.

His thoughts drifted to General Canton. He'd been trying to figure out why Belinda and Adelade brought Canton back to the lodge, and an idea had sprouted. It could be that Canton had hid the troop report before they left to go find Eldrida Petrie. If so, the belles needed him to find it for them. But that didn't explain why they took him with them when they left. It would have been simpler to shoot him.

Fatigue set in and Fargo found himself yawning.

Nothing moved in the reeds but he doubted Cain had left. When the monstrosity made up his mind to kill someone, he didn't stop until he did.

About three hours before dawn, Fargo woke Hosiah. He had to shake him several times to rouse him.

"Already?" Hosiah said. "I feel like I just closed my eyes."

Fargo needed to close his. He was bone weary. Without sleep he'd be useless. Fortunately, when his head touched the floor he was out like a snuffed wick. The next he knew, Hosiah was shaking him.

"Rise and shine, friend. The sun is about to play peekaboo with creation."

Fargo was sore and sluggish, his mind in a fog. He put coffee on and when it was hot gulped a cup.

Hosiah woke his brother and offered him some.

Wayland grimaced as he sat up. "I've been out all night? Did anything happen?"

"Not much," Fargo said.

Hosiah inspected the bandage. "There's no more blood. And it doesn't look infected. How do you feel?"

"Mad," Wayland said. "I want to find whoever knifed me and stick a blade into them."

"I am with you in that," Hosiah said.

Fargo was by the window, where he could see the horses. To reach the road they had to take the trail through the reeds.

And get past Cain Petrie.

32

The sun was above the horizon and the bright light of the new day had dispelled the last of night's shadows when Fargo and the Wilkes brothers stepped into their stirrups.

"I'll go first," Fargo said. "Keep your six-gun in your hand and if you shoot, go for the head."

"I know how to kill somebody," Wayland said.

"Do as he says," Hosiah told him. "You haven't fought the critter like we have. Lead doesn't seem to do more than sting the thing."

Fargo gigged the Ovaro.

The reeds swayed slightly to a wind out of the northwest. Where at night they were a black wall, in broad daylight they offered scant concealment for someone as huge as Cain Petrie.

Fargo rode ready. The creature—he couldn't quite think of Cain as entirely human—had nearly killed him twice now. The third time might be Cain's charm.

"It's downright sad about that poor Petrie gal," Wayland remarked. "Her own brother rippin' her head off like you say he done."

"Get her out of your head," Hosiah said, "and think about not lettin' that critter do the same to you."

The reeds practically brushed Fargo legs. They were only as high as his saddle and he could see down into them. Cain would have to be well hidden to escape notice.

The trail wound like a snake. Twice Fargo spotted real ones slithering off. That was encouraging. They wouldn't be crawling around if Cain were there.

He didn't breathe easy, though, until the reeds ended and they rode out into the open.

"Hallelujah," Hosiah exclaimed as they emerged. "That critter must have gone somewhere else."

"Too bad," Wayland said. "I'd like to put a few holes in his skull for what he did to Miss Petrie."

At the road Fargo dismounted. The most recent tracks, those of Belinda and Adelade and Canton, bore to the south, deeper into swamp county, and toward New Orleans.

"With any luck we'll catch them by sundown," Hosiah said as their pursuit began in earnest.

"Can't wait to pay them back for knifin' me," Wayland said.

"You know, brother," Hosiah said. "You're a hellion when it comes to blood for blood."

"As if you're not," Wayland said.

Fargo looked over his shoulder. "Do you two hear that?"

"Hear what?" Hosiah said.

"All I heard was us talkin'," Wayland said.

"That's all I heard, too," Fargo said.

"Oh," Hosiah said.

"Of course he'd hear us talkin'," Wayland said. "What did he mean by that?"

"It's his way of sayin' we should shut up," Hosiah said.

"Well, hell," Wayland said. "No one's ever accused me of bein' a jabber mouth before."

"They probably couldn't get a word in," Fargo said.

"Ha, ha," Wayland said, but he fell quiet and stayed so until they drew rein at noon to rest their mounts.

"We're pushin' pretty hard but still ain't caught up to them."

"They're pushin' pretty hard too," Hosiah said.

On both sides of the road swamp stretched into the distance. Brooding cypress loomed over sinister pools where ripples and bubbles hinted at lurkers below. Shadows writhed as if alive and the gay warbles of songbirds were seldom heard.

The gloom did nothing to improve Fargo's estimation of swamps. Why people lived in them, he'd never know.

They had encountered no one else all morning. But soon after starting out again, they rounded a bend and came on a wagon. A wiry oldster with an unkempt beard had lost a wheel and his load of hides—everything from coon to bobcat to bear—had nearly spilled out.

"Am I glad to see you gents," he said as they came to a stop. "How about lendin' me a hand puttin' this wheel back on?"

Fargo didn't mind. "Tell me, old-timer," he said as he put his back to the wagon to lift. "Have you seen anyone else come this way today?"

"Some feller and a couple of gals," the trapper answered. "Weren't more than an hour ago. I asked them to help but one of the females told me they were in a hurry. I said I could be stuck here for days if they didn't and she said she didn't give a good damn about an old goat like me."

"One of the women said that?" Hosiah said.

The trapper nodded. "An uppity thing with hair the color of gold. She was pretty but mean."

"What did the man say?" Fargo asked.

"Not one word. He was a mite peculiar."

"How so?"

"Well, he was ridin' ahead of them, so naturally I asked him first. Damned if he didn't look at the females as if he needed their say-so to answer me. And when the mean one told me no, he looked as if he was goin' to say somethin' but didn't have the gumption. He must be one of those henpecked fellas."

"Or something," Fargo said.

"Did those females say anythin' else?" Hosiah asked.

"As they were ridin' off I heard the other gal say as how she couldn't wait to get to New Orleans on account of she was tired of all the bugs and snakes and such."

"That's a city gal for you," Wayland said.

"Don't I know it, sonny?" the trapper said. "I lived with a city girl once. About drove me to pullin' my hair out. All she cared about was clothes and how she looked and what other people thought of her."

"Give me a country gal any day," Hosiah said.

"How about you, mister?" the trapper asked Fargo. "What kind of gals are you partial to?"

"Naked ones," Fargo said.

The old man was still chuckling to himself when they rode on.

Fargo was tempted to spur to a trot but the heat and the humidity would soon take a toll on their mounts. Better to conserve them for when their quarry came in sight.

Half an hour passed and Fargo grew increasingly anxious for a glimpse of the general. Again and again he rose in the stirrups but the road ahead was empty.

Then Wayland Wilkes hollered for them to stop, and when they did, he stared intently to the north.

"What is it?" Hosiah asked. "What did you see?"

"I thought . . ." Wayland said, and shook his head. "No. It couldn't be. My eyes must have been playin' tricks."

"Tell us anyway," Fargo said.

"I saw somethin'," Wayland said. "Somethin' big"—he pointed—"crossin' into that thicket, yonder."

"You're not sayin'—?" Hosiah began.

"I don't know," Wayland said. "It could have been. But it moved so fast, I couldn't be sure."

"It's still after us, as far as we've come?"

Fargo said, "He knows these swamps a lot better than we do. And we've had to stick to the road while he can cut straight through."

Hosiah sleeved his sweaty face. "God help us if you're right."

33

By the tracks, the women and the general were riding faster. They were suddenly in a hurry to get somewhere.

Fargo didn't know what to make of it. Here they were, literally in the middle of nowhere with nothing but swampland for mile after mile.

That soon changed. They came to a junction with another road, narrower and a lot less traveled.

"I didn't know this was here," Hosiah said.

"How would we?" Wayland said. "We ain't ever been this far south before."

The new road ran from east to west. To the east it disappeared into the swamp. To the west it would take them to woodland.

The tracks pointed west.

"They must be fixin' to stop for the night," Wayland said, "and those woods would be a handy place to hide."

"If'n they post a lookout, they'll see us," Hosiah said.

Fargo decided to take a gamble. He held to a walk, his hand on his Colt.

Behind him Wayland said, "Just so you know, mister, I'm shootin' those women the moment I set eyes on them."

"I'd like to talk to them first."

"It's important you do?"

"Important enough."

They were almost to the trees when Wayland drew rein and said, "Will you look at that? Don't often see them but up in the sky."

A pair of buzzards sat on a branch. Wings tucked, the carrion eaters showed no fear.

"I hope they're not an omen," Hosiah said.

"Ugly birds is all they are," Wayland said. "I'd shoot 'em if it wouldn't give us away."

"You'd shoot anythin'," Hosiah said. "Remember that time you plunked a bluebird? Prettiest birds there are and you kilt it for no reason."

"How about if I leave you here so you can talk birds to your heart's content?" Fargo broke in.

"Sorry," Hosiah said.

Shadows enveloped them. Fargo figured to find the women and Canton camped in a clearing but the day had another surprise in store.

The oaks and other trees thinned and a knoll rose. Half an acre in extent, its flat top was crowned by the last thing Fargo expected to find: a cabin.

"I'll be switched," Wayland whispered as they drew rein.

Three familiar horses were tied out front and smoke curled from the stone chimney.

"Whose place can it be?" Hosiah said. "That trapper we ran into?"

Fargo doubted it. He hadn't seen any wagon ruts. Dismounting, he wrapped the reins and shucked the Henry. Moving to a larger tree, he hunkered down.

"What are we waitin' for?" Wayland said. "I say we barge on in and take 'em by surprise."

"Use your head," Hosiah said. "They could be peekin' out that window and us not know it."

"I ain't one for patience," Wayland said.

Fargo was close to losing his. "Do either of you have a needle and thread?"

"What do you need them for?" Wayland asked.

"To sew your damn mouth shut."

"Hey now."

To reach the cabin they'd have to cross thirty feet of open space. Perfect targets for anyone inside.

"Stay put," Fargo said, and circled to see if there was a back door. No such luck. Back around front, he squatted behind the same tree.

The brothers were looking at him, waiting for him to say what to do. By unspoken consent, they were following his lead.

"Well?" Wayland prompted.

"Cover me," Fargo said. "I'm going to try to see what they're up to." Flattening, he crawled. He moved quickly once he was in the open, expecting a shout or a shot. He reached the cabin, rose into a crouch, and sidled to the window. The glass was thick with dust. He inched an eye to a corner. It took a few seconds for things to come into focus.

Adelade sat at a small table, spooning stew from a bowl. Two other bowls had been set out, along with spoons.

Fargo didn't see the general or Belinda. He shifted for a better view of the rest of the room. He thought he'd find Canton bound and a prisoner. But no.

General Thaddeus Canton and Belinda were seated on a bench. They were talking and smiling as if they were the best of friends.

Fargo lowered his head before Adelade spotted him. Shock hit him like a punch to the gut. It raised a host of questions. Scowling, he moved to the door. He gripped the wooden latch, girded himself, and threw the door wide open. Springing inside, he leveled the Henry and said, "Knock, knock."

Adelade froze with a spoon halfway to her mouth.

Over on the bench, Belinda started to reach for her handbag, which was on the floor at her feet.

"Give me an excuse," Fargo said.

Belinda turned to stone.

As for Thaddeus Canton, he sat back and smiled and said casually, "Well, Skye. Aren't you the persistent devil."

"General," Fargo said. "You have some explaining to do."

"Do I, indeed?" Canton said good-naturedly. "Yes, I suppose I do. But first I must know. How did you find us?"

"I tracked you."

"How else?" Canton said, and laughed. "Only you could have. Your reputation as one of the best trackers alive isn't an exaggeration."

Belinda looked at Adelade. "I told you we shouldn't underestimate him."

"Yes, you did," Adelade said. She was flushed with anger and glaring venomously at Fargo. "And I told you at the lodge that we should wait for Hosiah and him to return and dispose of them but you wouldn't listen. You were in too much of a hurry."

"We have an appointment to keep, remember?" Belinda said.

"That we do, my dear," General Canton said, looking at Fargo. "One I would very much like to not be interfered with."

"What appointment?" Fargo said.

Adelade smiled her cat-eyed smile. "As if we'd tell you. You'd have been smart to let us go. Following us was the stupidest thing you could have done."

"He's never struck me as stupid," Belinda remarked. To Fargo she said, "Prove me right. Switch sides, and when we get to New Orleans, I'll make it well worth your while."

"No, thanks," Fargo said.

"Then you are a fool," Belinda said. "You think you have the upper hand but you don't."

"This is far from over," Adelade said. "Pretty soon I expect only one of us will still be breathing." She grinned. "Can you guess who?"

34

Fargo was amazed at her confidence. Before he could say anything, boots drummed and into the cabin burst Hosiah and Wayland. They drew up short and trained their rifles.

"You were takin' too long," the latter said.

"We reckoned you might be in trouble," Hosiah said.

The general smiled. "The gang's all here, as they way. Welcome, gentlemen. Have a seat, why don't you? There's plenty of stew for all."

"What the hell?" Wayland said.

"You must have ridden hard to overtake us," Canton said. "Surely you're hungry and could use some rest?"

"What are you up to?" Hosiah said.

"Nothing. Nothing at all," the general replied.

"Check them for weapons," Fargo said.

The Wilkes brothers eagerly complied. After making Adelade stand, Wayland patted every square inch of her body. She endured the treatment with icy contempt. "Nothin' on her," he said.

Hosiah was careful not to get between Fargo and the general and Belinda as he frisked each. He relieved Canton of the revolver in his shoulder holster and found a pistol in Belinda's handbag. "That's all there is."

Canton said. "You should feel perfectly safe now. How about some stew?"

"Don't mind if I do," Wayland said. He shooed Adelade away from the table, straddled her chair, and commenced to eat from her bowl. "Not bad," he said. "But it could use more salt."

"How you can think of food at a time like this is beyond me," Hosiah said.

"What about you?" Canton said to Fargo. "Care to partake?"

"All I want," Fargo said, "is to know why."

The general leaned back. "What is usually the case in instances like this? Money. Lots and lots of money." He roved his gaze over Belinda. "Plus other rewards."

"You've been with the other side all along?"

"Not at all," Canton said. "When I first met you at the inn, I was fully committed to performing my duty and seeing that the secret report is delivered into the hands of the president."

"What happened?" Fargo asked. As if he couldn't guess.

"*I* happened," Belinda said fiercely. "I made him see that what he was doing was wrong. Thaddeus was born and raised in the South. He has Southern sensibilities. I convinced him that his real duty is to the land and the people he was born into, not to a bunch of Yankees who think they have the right to play God."

"Hold on," Hosiah said. "What's this secret report business?"

Belinda latched onto his question like a hound dog onto a bone. "It's why you and your brother should be on our side and not his." She nodded at Fargo. "If you help him best us, you're hurting the South and everything you hold dear."

Wayland had stopped eating. "What in hell are you talkin' about, lady?"

"The coming war between the North and the South," Belinda said. "Surely you're aware that the new president has demanded we change our ways or he will go to war? Surely you've heard that certain Southern states are thinking of seceding from the Union?"

"I've heard some such," Hosiah said, "but what's that got to do with us helpin' the scout?"

"He's working for the Yankees," Belinda said. "He brought a secret dispatch to General Canton. A troop report that could help the South greatly when war breaks out. The general was to pass it on to his superiors but he's had a change of heart."

"That I have, boys," Canton said.

"Point your rifle at the scout and not at us," Belinda urged Hosiah. "He's your real enemy."

Wayland shifted his chair to face her. "Nice try, bitch."

"How dare you," Belinda said indignantly.

"It weren't Fargo who stabbed me in the back and left me for dead," Wayland said. "It was one of you females. Or maybe Thaddeus."

Fargo hadn't thought of that. He'd assumed Belinda or Adelade was responsible.

"Which?" Wayland said.

"We didn't want to," Belinda said.

"We were only doing our duty," Adelade threw in.

Wayland asked again, "Which?"

"Don't tell him," General Canton said.

"Stabbin' me ain't all you have to answer for," Wayland said. "Or have you forgot slittin' our brother's throat?" He put down the spoon and rose. "I should kill all three of you here and now."

"You have your gall askin' us to side with you," Hosiah said to Belinda. "We're Southerners, sure. You're right about that. But for us, kin counts for more than anything else."

"You can go to hell, both you bitches," Wayland said.

Belinda grew red in the face and went to say something but Canton grasped her arm.

"Don't bother, my dear. You'd only waste your breath. These two aren't capable of putting the greater good above their own. It's a shame."

"They'll have to be dealt with, the same as Fargo," Adelade said.

"Dealt with?" Fargo said.

Belinda smiled. "We certainly can't let you live. You'd report the general, and now that I've helped him see the light, I want him to go on helping the South. Secretly, of course."

"Isn't she wonderful?" Canton said.

"It occurred to me," Belinda continued, "that instead of stealing the report, it would better serve our cause if we copy it and let the general deliver the original. Then he can go on relaying important information to those leading the Southern cause."

"As a spy," Adelade said. "Like us."

Belinda nodded. "Think of it. He'll be in the inner circle of Yankee commanders. I expect he can help turn the early tide of the war. Perhaps even win it for our side."

"You and that stupid war," Wayland said. "You keep forgettin' you have me and Abimelech to answer for."

"Simpleton," Adelade said "We'd do it again for the cause. We'll do anything to see that the South prevails."

"We've stalled long enough," Belinda said. "And I don't like having guns pointed at me."

"Stalled?" Fargo said.

Hosiah swung his rifle toward Belinda. "You can stall all you want but you're still as good as dead."

"Silly man," Belinda said. "I'll say this only once. You and your brother and Mr. Fargo are to lay your weapons on the floor. Do it nice and slow and raise your hands in the air."

"Silly cow," Wayland mimicked her. "Why should we?"

"Because if you don't," Belinda said, "the men behind you will shoot you to ribbons."

"Nice bluff," Wayland said, and laughed.

"No," said a hard voice behind Fargo. "It isn't."

35

Fargo started to turn and caught himself.

Four men were crowded at the doorway, pointing rifles. At the window were two more. Their rifles were cocked and their expressions left no doubt they would do as they threatened.

"I'd listen to the lady, gents," said the same man, who was dressed as the rest in ordinary clothes that could be bought at any general store. He had blond hair and a blond mustache and an accent that hinted at Georgia or the Carolinas. He also wore a Smith & Wesson slantwise across his hip for a cross draw.

Wayland had set his rifle on the table and began to reach for it.

"Are you that eager to die, boy?" the blond man said. "We'll drop you, as sure as anything."

"Wayland, no," Hosiah said.

Belinda put her hands on her hips. "Your weapons. I won't tell you again."

Fargo wasn't about to commit suicide. He set down the Henry, plucked the Colt from his holster using two fingers, and lowered it to the floor.

Hosiah was doing the same with his rifle. "Wayland, damn it. Don't you dare."

His brother had hesitated. But now, with an oath, Wayland took hold of his rifle by the stock. Instead of lowering it, he threw it at Adelade.

She barely caught it before it struck her face. Glowering, she trained it on him. "I'll splatter your brains, you bastard. You should have died when I stabbed you. Your brother went quick when I slit his stupid throat."

"So it was you," Wayland said.

"Leave the splattering to Captain Fletcher," Belinda said, and turned to the blond man. "About time you got here. You were supposed to be waiting for us."

"It's a long ride from New Orleans," the man called Fletcher drawled. "We pushed our horses as hard as we dared."

"You're here now, Captain. That's what counts. We can dispose of these three and wrap this up."

"Yes, ma'am," Captain Fletcher said. "And what about him?" He gestured at Canton.

"The good general has had a change of heart," Belinda said. "I appealed to the Southerner in him and he decided to come over to our side. You won't need to kill him as we originally planned."

"You don't say," Captain Fletcher said.

Fargo's attention was solely on the rifles pointed at him. "You're in the army, too?"

"You remember me then?" Fletcher said.

Fargo looked at him. The man's face tugged vaguely at his memory. "I feel like I should."

"We met once down to Fort Bowie," Captain Fletcher said. "You were sent to help track down some Apaches. You worked with the colonel, not with me. He introduced us, was all."

"And here you are working against your own government," Fargo said.

"I'm against that no-good Lincoln and those like him who think they have the right to tell the South how we should live," Fletcher drawled. "From the day big ears was elected, I've set myself to doing all I can to stop him."

"Captain Fletcher is one of our top spies," Belinda boasted. "He's passed us a lot of crucial information, just as General Canton will now do."

"I do what I can," Fletcher said with pride.

"Where's your uniform?" Fargo asked.

"Hanging in the closet of my hotel room in New Orleans. I don't want everyone to know what I am, now do I?"

Fargo glanced at the others. "Are they soldiers too?"

"Only me," Fletcher said. "These are good old Southern boys, loyal to the cause."

General Canton cleared his throat. "Am I to surmise that it was you who somehow found out about the secret troop report and let these ladies know?"

"I reported it to those in charge of our efforts," Fletcher said, "and they assigned Belinda and Adelade to take it from you."

"So the three of you aren't in command?"

"What gave you that idea?" Captain Fletcher said. "We're middling level. Those we take orders from are higher up." He smirked. "And a lot closer to the president."

"You don't say," Canton said.

"Enough talk," Adelade snapped. "Take the scout and these other two out and shoot them."

"No," Captain Fletcher said.

"I'll remind you that you're supposed to work with us," Adelade said, "not boss us around."

"And I'll remind you that we were told not to arouse suspicion," Fletcher said. "If we shoot Fargo and his body is found, the Yankees will investigate."

"It won't be found if you bury him," Adelade said.

"Why risk it when there's a better way?" Captain Fletcher argued. "We find a rattlesnake and have it bite him. Then we'll leave his body where it will be found so the snake is blamed and no one is the wiser."

"Why, Captain, that's brilliant," Belinda said.

"A grisly way to go," General Canton remarked.

"Not as grisly as tossing him in quicksand would be," Captain Fletcher said. "Which, come to think of it, will work fine for these other two."

"You would do that to two boys from the South?" Hosiah said.

"I am plumb sorry," Fletcher said. "But unless you renounce the North and join our cause, you're as much an enemy as any Yankee."

"We'll gladly join you," Hosiah said. "Won't we, Wayland?"

Wayland was glowering at Adelade and didn't respond.

Captain Fletcher sighed and said to Hosiah, "I'd like to take you at your word. But I overheard you about your brother and I suspect neither of you can forgive and forget." He paused. "Southerners or not, you and your brother, and the scout, will be in hell before this day is done."

36

Fargo had to submit to being hauled from the cabin, bound hand and foot, and left lying on his side with the Wilkes brothers. The five men with Fletcher stayed outside watching them while the captain went in to confer with the women and General Canton.

"Ain't this a fine mess?" Wayland said in disgust.

"It makes me sick to my stomach, a Southern boy turnin' against his own kind," Hosiah said.

The thing that rankled Fargo was the general turning traitor. The brass in Washington probably thought they were doing the right thing when they chose Canton because he was born and bred in those parts. It never occurred to them that Canton might put the South's interests above their own.

"Do you feel that?" Hosiah abruptly asked.

"Feels like rain on the way," Wayland said.

Fargo raised his head. They were right. The wind had picked up and turned cooler, and to the west a scuttling bank of dark clouds promised a storm would strike within the hour.

Wayland struggled with his binds until one of the Southerners came over and kicked him.

"That'll be enough of that, mister."

"You can go to hell," Wayland said, "and take the bitch who killed our brother with you."

The man walked off muttering about "jackasses."

"You oughtn't to provoke them," Hosiah warned. "It doesn't do you any good to make them mad."

"We're goin' to be killed any minute now," Wayland said. "Who cares if they're mad or not?"

Fargo inched his fingers down his pant leg. He tried to pry the rope around his ankles loose so he could slip his fingers into his boot and palm the Arkansas toothpick but the knots were too tight.

"This is a hell of a way to meet our end," Hosiah said. "Killed by our own kind."

"Our kind, hell," Wayland said. "The only thing we have in common is they're from the South. But so what? They claim they're riled at the Yankees for wantin' to make war on us, yet here they are, makin' war on you and me and we're as Southern bred as they are."

"I hadn't thought of it like that," Hosiah said.

"It's the only way to think of it," Wayland said. "When a man says he's fightin' for the South and then claims it calls for him to make worm food of a pair of Southern boys like us, he's talkin' out both sides of his mouth at once."

Fargo went on prying. He'd figured that Captain Fletcher would want to get it over with right away but the palaver in the cabin was taking a good long while. If he could think of a way to free himself and the Wilkes brothers before Fletcher was done, there would be hell to pay.

A gust of wind fanned his face. The tops of nearby trees bent and in the far distance thunder rumbled.

"That storm could be a godsend," Hosiah said while regarding the oncoming clouds.

"How so?" Wayland asked.

"You heard the captain. They want Fargo to die of snake bite. And for us, it's quicksand."

"So?"

"So use your noggin. What do a lot of snakes do when it rains?"

"They hunt cover," Wayland said. "They don't like the cold and the wet."

"Fletcher will have to wait until after the storm is over to go lookin' for them. And I can't see him ridin' around in a storm huntin' for quicksand, neither."

Just then Captain Fletcher and Belinda strode from the cabin. Fletcher studied the clouds and the bending trees and said, "This will delay things."

"It shouldn't last long," Belinda said. "They never do."

"I want to be on our way to New Orleans."

"So do I. But it can't be helped. You and your men should eat and rest, and as soon as the rain stops, we'll finish this."

Hosiah bent toward his brother and whispered, "I told you so."

"An extra hour doesn't do us much good if we can't get free," Wayland stated the obvious.

Fargo continued to try. His fingers hurt like blazes and it felt as if he might rip his fingernails off, but he pried and pried. He stopped when Captain Fletcher walked over.

"I reckon you heard. You might want to spend the extra time making peace with your Maker."

"When did you become a parson?" Wayland asked in contempt.

"You have a mouth on you, boy," Captain Fletcher said, "and precious little common sense."

"At least I ain't no traitor."

"You can't mean me. I'm the one fighting for the South. All you care about is your own hide."

"My hide is as Southern as yours," Wayland said. "Which makes you—what do they call it? A hypocrite."

"I wouldn't expect you to understand," Captain Fletcher said. "I bet you can't even read or write."

"What's that got to do with anything?"

"He's sayin' you're dumb," Hosiah said.

"You both are, going against the express wishes of those of us who have rallied to the South's cause," Captain Fletcher said.

"Highfalutin words don't make you right and us wrong," Wayland said. "You're still full of horseshit."

"I'm wasting my time talking to you." Doing an about-face, Captain Fletcher returned to Belinda.

"What did that accomplish?" Hosiah asked his brother.

"I put him in his place, didn't I?"

Miles off, lightning rent the heavens. Fargo counted the seconds and got to five before he heard thunder. The storm was still a ways off.

Inside the cabin, Adelade hollered that the stew was dished out and for the men to come get some. Belinda and Fletcher and three of the men went in. The other two stayed by the door.

"Too bad they didn't go eat, too," Wayland said.

"They're not dumb," Hosiah said. "They won't leave us unguarded."

A shriek keened the air at the strongest gust yet. Tree limbs whipped in a frenzy. Somewhere a branch broke with a loud crack and there was the crash of it falling to earth.

A few light drops heralded the downpour to come.

"I suppose they're just goin' to let us lie out here and get soaked," Wayland complained.

Fargo didn't mind. The rain might loosen the ropes. Enough that he could at last get to the toothpick.

Another crash drew his gaze to the forest. The scuttling clouds had plunged everything into shadow. Pretty soon it would be so dark as to be like night.

Suddenly Fargo stiffened. One of the shadows had moved. An enormous shape, unmistakable as anyone or anything other than who it was.

Cain Petrie had found them.

37

Fargo was the only one who noticed. He wanted to warn the Wilkeses but the two guards chose that moment to come over.

"What do you gents want?" Wayland said.

"We're moving you closer to the cabin," one replied, "so we can keep an eye on you when the rain starts."

They took Hosiah first, each sliding a hand under his arm and hauling him none too gently.

"I'll kick their knees out," Wayland said, drawing his legs to his chest.

"And be shot for nothing," Fargo said.

"They aim to throw us in quicksand, remember?" Waylon said, but he lowered his legs.

More thunder pealed. The wind buffeted them. Fargo looked for Cain Petrie but didn't see him.

The guards seized Waylon. He grumbled but didn't resist.

Fargo had taken his eyes off the forest. He didn't hear anything unusual and was stunned when an enormous arm wrapped around him and he was lifted off the ground. He tried to turn and was cuffed on the head. Pain exploded and his vision swam. He was aware of moving swiftly. He heard shouts and a rifle blasted.

Cain Petrie had taken him right out from under the noses of the rebels. It was a case of not just going from the frying pan into a fire but from the pan into an inferno.

Fargo shook his head to clear it, marveling at how effortlessly the outcast carried him.

Cain's bear hide stank to high heaven, and Cain himself was no bouquet. If cleanliness was next to godliness, as the saying had it, then Cain was as far from godly as a person could get.

The Southerners were giving chase but it was too late.

The storm broke in all its elemental ferocity. Rain fell in a deluge and the wind was a banshee.

Fargo struggled and received another cuff. His ears rang and his head was pure torment but he didn't black out. He wondered what Cain had in mind, and thought of Eldrida. It made his neck itch.

The wilds were a bedlam of wind and breaking limbs and the heavy panting of Cain Petrie in Fargo's ear. He didn't try to break free. Two cuffs were enough. Another might split his head open.

The abomination stopped and threw Fargo to the ground. There was no forewarning. Fargo tried to bear the brunt on his shoulder but he was only halfway around when he struck and his side and right leg spiked with agony and then his leg went numb.

Cain Petrie bent over him.

Now what? Fargo thought. He stayed perfectly still as Petrie's huge hands poked and probed. Looking for weapons, Fargo figured.

A bolt of lightning lit their surroundings. Fargo glimpsed a bank, and water, and realized Cain had brought him to the edge of the swamp.

Fargo became drenched. He blinked to try to keep the rain out of his eyes but it was hopeless.

A huge hand closed on his throat and Fargo reckoned his time had come. He kicked Cain and threw himself back, or tried to. The hand around his throat pinned him with the same ease he would pin an infant.

Cain Petrie bent lower.

"What do you want?" Fargo shouted to be heard above the storm, knowing it was useless. He might as well have asked the wind.

Cain straightened. He looked at the turbulent sky and gestured as if he were annoyed. Then he wheeled and disappeared into the rain.

Fargo didn't waste a moment. He rolled away from the swamp, rolled and rolled until he collided with a tree. Wriggling around it, he rolled some more. In no time he was covered with muck and mud. He went on rolling.

When he had gone far enough to feel safe, he worked at the rope around his ankles. As he'd hoped, the rope moved a little when he tugged. Not much, but by working it back and forth and from side to side, he was slowly able to slide it lower so he could free his pant leg and slide his hand into his boot.

The Arkansas toothpick blade made short shrift of his bonds. Rising, he flexed his legs and arms to restore circulation.

Now to help the Wilkeses. The only problem was that he couldn't get his bearings. Was he east of the cabin? West of it? North or South? Without the sun or the stars to guide him, he was as lost as any greenhorn.

Another bolt rent the sky and a tree was split down the middle.

The strike was so close that his hair stood on end and his skin prickled as from a thousand tiny pins.

The two halves of the tree crashed down.

Fargo ran. He hadn't taken three strides when there was a tremendous thud behind him and something brushed his shoulder. Stopping, he discovered that one of the halves had missed him by a whisker.

He went to go around and came to where several limbs were tangled together, forming a bower that offered some protection from Nature's tantrum. He ducked under it and hunkered down.

Fargo figured to wait out the storm and then go deal with General Canton and the Southerners.

The pelting raindrops sounded like hail.

Fargo folded his forearms across his knees and placed his chin on his wrist. He was comfortable enough, given the circumstances.

Then something moved off in the rain, something huge.

Cain Petrie was back—and hunting for him.

38

Fargo held his breath without realizing he was doing it. Cain wasn't more than four or five feet away, turning from side to side. Cain's back was to the tree.

After a seeming eternity, the hulking shape melted away.

Fargo let out a breath. He could relax for a while, until the storm ended.

He couldn't get over that General Canton had turned traitor. It suggested that a lot of people living south of the Mason-Dixon Line would rally to the Southern cause when and if war did break out. He'd hate to see that happen. It would split the country down the middle, pit brother against brother, friend against friend.

The pelting rain showed no sign of slacking.

Fargo pulled his hat brim lower to prevent drops from splashing onto his face. He was clammy and cold and would dearly love a fire and a pot of coffee.

The lightning and thunder stopped but the rain went on.

Fargo was about convinced he'd have to endure a miserably wet night when the downpour dwindled to a drizzle. The sky went from black to gray, which told him the sun hadn't set yet.

The drizzle ended. The clouds began to disperse and random shafts of sunlight broke through. Steam rose, adding to the humidity.

Fargo poked his head out from under the bower. He saw no sign of Cain Petrie. Judging from the position of the sun, he was west of the cabin. Cautiously easing out, he bent his steps toward it.

The forest was alive with noise: the patter of dripping drops, the cries and chirps of birds, the chatter of a squirrel.

Fargo made for where he and the Wilkes brothers had left their horses, intending to move them before the Southerners found them. To his consternation, the animals were gone. He looked for tracks but the rain had washed them away.

Fargo fought down a surge of panic. One of his secret fears was that one day the Ovaro would be stolen or come to harm. About to go on, he heard voices, and crouched.

Several figures were approaching.

Fargo thought they were after him and yearned for his Colt.

One of them was saying, ". . . can they have gotten to? We don't find them, we'll be stuck here."

They? Fargo wondered.

"Quit fretting," said another. "They were spooked by the storm, is all, and ran off."

"We'll find them eventually," said a third.

Fargo realized they were searching for their horses, not for him.

"We'd better find them soon," said the first. "I don't like these woods. They're too damn spooky."

"Will you listen to yourself?" said the second.

"How old are you? Ten?" mocked the third.

Fargo saw them, hiking abreast with rifles. They weren't wet except for their boots.

"I tell you I saw something out the window," the first one said. "And it wasn't the scout, either."

"You can't be sure who or what it was," the second man said. "It was raining like hell."

"It was too big to be him," the first insisted.

"A bear, then," suggested the third. "No wonder the horses ran off."

"If we don't find them, that murderous little bitch Adelade will raise a fuss."

"I don't like her one bit."

"Belinda is nice. Her and the captain get along right fine."

They passed out of earshot.

Fargo rose and stalked toward the cabin. He had to get the Wilkeses out of there.

Circling, he came up on it from the east. The last fifty feet he snaked on his belly. A peek around the corner showed a guard by the front door. Past the guard, along the wall, lay the brothers, still bound but alive.

Hosiah looked glum. Wayland, as usual, looked angry.

Fargo was debating whether to lure the guard closer and jump him when the stillness was shattered by several shots from the vicinity of where he had seen the three men.

The guard took a few steps and stopped.

Out of the cabin rushed Captain Fletcher with Belinda and Adelade close behind him.

"It must be Jeffords and the others," the guard said. "They ran into some kind of trouble."

"But what?" Belinda said.

As if in answer there was a tremendous roar.

"Not that monster again!" Adelade exclaimed.

Captain Fletcher drew his Smith & Wesson. "The thing you were telling us about? The Night Terror?"

"That's him," Belinda said.

General Canton emerged. He clasped his hands behind his back as if at parade rest and said, "Now we know what happened to our horses. You'd better go see to your men, Captain, before it's too late."

Fletcher gestured at the guard. "Come with me. Ladies, watch our prisoners until we get back." He broke into a jog, saying over his shoulder, "If we're not back by dawn, we're dead."

"You will be," Belinda called after him.

Adelade smirked and said, "Getting attached, are we?"

Belinda gave her a pointed look. "He's a friend, is all."

Hosiah Wilkes rose on an elbow. "What about us? You can't leave us lyin' here with that critter on the loose."

"Sure we can," Adelade said. "It might save us the trouble of killing you ourselves."

Fargo coiled his legs. The women had left their rifles inside, and Canton's revolver was in his shoulder holster. He'd never have a better chance. He started to rise—just as a hard object poked him in the back and someone said, "Give me an excuse and you're dead."

39

Fargo had forgotten there were six Southerners, counting Fletcher. He slowly turned his head and stared into the muzzle of a rifle.

The man holding it was grinning. "Didn't think we had a look-out out back, did you? I saw you sneakin' up."

"Damn," Fargo said.

The man chuckled. "I'd feel stupid, too. How about if you crawl on around and we'll join the rest."

"Crawl?"

"Try to stand and I'll shoot you."

Fargo crawled.

Adelade saw him, and laughed. Belinda let out a startled gasp and pulled a pocket pistol from her handbag. General Canton frowned.

"Well, look who it is, brother," Wayland Wilkes said. "Our pard has come to rescue us."

"Some rescue," Hosiah said.

Adelade walked over and without any hint of her intentions, kicked Fargo in the side. "That's for getting away. But you won't this time."

Fargo realized they had no idea that Cain Petrie had taken him.

Adelade wasn't done. She drew back her foot to kick him again. "And this is for being Yankee scum."

"Don't," Belinda said.

Adelade looked at her, puzzled. "Give me one good reason why not."

"We tie him first," Belinda said. "He might try something."

"I'd like to see him," the man with the rifle said.

Adelade lowered her foot. "Fine, Belinda. You want him helpless so we can do as we please. I'll go you one better."

"How do you mean?" Belinda asked.

"I want him dead." Adelade slid her left hand up her right sleeve and drew a pearl-hilted dagger. "See this?" she said to the Wilkes brothers. "It's what I used to slit Abimelech's throat."

"Why, you—" Wayland growled, and attempted to sit up.

Adelade bent, knocked Fargo's hat off, and gripped a handful of hair. "I like sitting throats. It's quiet and easy and they die quick." Wrenching his head back, she held the dagger close to his neck. "Any last words?"

"Just do it," Belinda said.

"She prefers to play cat and mouse, I would imagine," General Canton said. "A shame, really, that she has to spoil things."

"The only thing I'm spoiling is his life," Adelade said.

"I beg to differ, woman," General Canton said, moving his hand under his jacket. "You've spoiled what I thought was a very clever plan, if I say so, myself."

"I don't know what in hell you're talking about," Adelade said.

"In that case," General Canton said, "perhaps I can make myself more clear." He drew his Starr revolver and shot Adelade in the face, shifted, and shot the astonished guard in the forehead. Belinda cried out and swung toward him and he struck her across the temple, dropping her where she stood.

"What the hell?" Wayland blurted.

Fargo was speechless with bewilderment.

"Here you go, Skye," Canton said, extending his other hand to help Fargo to his feet. "I wish you hadn't let yourself be caught. All my effort has been for naught."

"General," Hosiah said, "are you sayin' you're on our side again?"

"I was never on the other side." Canton peered into the trees. "We'll have to move quickly. They'll have heard the shots and come on the run."

"I'm obliged for killing her," Fargo said, "but I'll be damned if I know why you did it."

"First things first," Canton said. "You'll find your six-shooter and rifle on the table. I advise you to fetch them and help me free the Wilkeses so we can get out of here."

"I like that idea," Wayland said.

Fargo went in. His weapons were where Canton had said they would be. He checked that the Colt was loaded and twirled it into his holster, then jacked a round into the Henry's chamber.

"Hurry," the general urged.

Off in the woods, someone was shouting Belinda's name. Fletcher, it sounded like.

Canton was untying Wayland.

Fargo drew his toothpick and with it cut Hosiah loose. "Your guns are inside, too."

Belinda groaned.

"We'll take her with us," General Canton said. "I might be able to salvage something from this debacle." He used the rope he removed from Wayland to tie her wrists behind her back but he left her legs free. "So we don't have to carry her," he explained.

The shouts were louder.

Canton quickly sat Belinda up and smacked her cheek. Once, twice, three hard slaps and she stirred and opened her eyes.

"What's going on?"

"In good time, my dear," Canton said. Hauling her erect, he gave her a shove. "Start running. I'd advise you not to cry out or I'll hit you a lot harder."

Belinda looked as confused as Fargo. She took several faltering steps and Canton shoved her again.

"Spare me your theatrics, woman," Canton said. "Move faster or else."

"I'm hurting, damn you," Belinda said. "I can barely think."

Canton pressed his revolver to her back. "In a very few moments you won't be able to breathe, either."

Belinda ran.

Fargo brought up the rear, with Wayland.

"Answer me true. Do you know what's goin' on?"

"I'm confused as hell," Fargo confessed.

"Good," Wayland said. "I wouldn't want to think it was just me."

40

The heat was sweltering, the humidity left them slick with sweat. They fled until Belinda staggered and announced she couldn't go another step.

Fargo believed her. He was winded himself.

"Very well, my dear," General Canton said. "You may stop under that willow, there."

Belinda collapsed in the shade and lay gasping for breath.

General Canton leaned against the trunk and put his hands on his knees. "Desk work doesn't keep a soldier very fit," he remarked.

"Your mouth works fine," Wayland said, "and I'd like to hear what in blazes is goin' on."

"It's simple," Canton replied.

"Says you," Hosiah said. "First you're with us and then you're against us and now you're with us again. What's simple about that?"

"I never left you. I only pretended to." General Canton coughed and mopped at his face.

"We're waiting," Fargo said.

Canton took off his hat and mopped at his hair, too. "I'd suspected that the two ladies were working for the secessionists. When they showed up at the Petrie hunting lodge, I was sure of it. That line they fed us about wanting our company to New Orleans was nonsense. They could have hired men in Haven to take them."

"I was suspicious, too," Fargo said.

"They didn't show their hand, though, until they stabbed Wayland. He and I were waiting for you to return and they crept up on us and Adelade stabbed Wayland before I knew what was happening."

"The bitch," Wayland interrupted.

"She got hers," Hosiah said.

"They demanded I hand the troop report over. I told them I couldn't. That I'd hidden it at the lodge."

"Did you?" Fargo asked.

"No. I had been concerned they might jump me and take the dispatch pouch, so I'd taken the report out and rolled it up in my bedroll. When I showed them the empty pouch, they believed me about hiding it at the lodge."

"Smart," Wayland said.

"They forced me to go back at gunpoint. The whole way, Belinda prattled on and on about how I should quit bowing down to my Yankee masters and join with her and her confederates in helping the South. I acted as if I was interested and she became excited and said I'd make a wonderful spy and could do their cause a world of good. I told her I'd think it over."

"Are all generals as sneaky as you?" Wayland asked.

"A few," Canton said.

"I wouldn't mind bein' a general my own self," Wayland said. "I can be sneaky as anybody."

"Will you let him finish?" Hosiah said.

"Thank you," Canton said. "We were almost to the lodge when Belinda mentioned that an army captain and some others were to meet them and escort them to New Orleans. I wanted to know who the captain was but I couldn't come right out and ask."

"So you played along to find out," Fargo guessed.

General Canton nodded. "Things went well until you showed up and got yourselves caught. Then when Adelade was set to cut your throat, I had to step in."

"Sorry we spoiled your plan," Hosiah said.

"It's not entirely ruined," Canton said, with a nod at Belinda. "She knows a lot more than she's revealed. I'll turn her over to be interrogated, and trust me when I say she'll reveal everything."

"Like hell I will," Belinda said.

Fargo checked their back trail. "We still have Fletcher and his men to deal with. And to find our horses." He wasn't leaving that swamp without the Ovaro.

"Don't forget that Petrie critter, too," Hosiah said.

"We can lick the whole passel," Wayland declared. "We have our guns and we're in one piece."

"I'd like to stay that way," Hosiah said.

General Canton said, "I was told that Fletcher has experience as a tracker. He's not as good as Fargo but then no one is."

"We'll let them find us," Fargo proposed. "Set a trap and end it."

"Trap where?" Wayland asked. "Here won't do. There aren't enough places to hide."

"We keep going," Fargo said. Sooner or later they would come across a likely spot. He went over to Belinda and pulled her to her feet. "I'll keep an eye on the lady spy for a while."

"Be my guest," General Canton said. "But watch her close."

Belinda pulled her arm from Fargo's grasp. "Keep your hands to yourself. You can make me do what you want but don't touch me."

"We're not good enough for you—is that it?" Hosiah said.

"You're scum," Belinda said.

"Don't sugarcoat it," Wayland said. "Tell us how you really feel."

"Go to hell."

Fargo pushed her. "You first. And remember we're right behind you."

Belinda stomped off but her fatigue soon caused her to slow. Her dress was a mess and her hair disheveled. "I hate this," she said.

"You brought it on yourself, my dear," Canton said.

"It's what I get for taking you at your word. You had me fooled. I believed you when you told us you'd had a change of heart."

"What's that expression?" the general said. "All's fair in love and war."

"There will be one, you know. A war. It's inevitable. That buffoon we have for a president has no right to dictate how the South should handle its own affairs. Slavery has been around for thousands of years. It'll be around for thousands more."

"Don't expect me to go fight a bunch of Yankees over a bunch of cotton pickers," Wayland said.

Belinda snorted. "I don't expect anything from you and your kind."

"I have a kind now?" Wayland said.

"You're a typical bumpkin. You have no interest in politics and don't care enough to resist Yankee oppression. It falls to people like Captain Fletcher and me, true patriots, to fight for our cause. You think you'll get away but you won't. Captain Fletcher and his men will make amends for my mistake."

"You sure are fond of hearin' yourself talk."

Hosiah laughed.

Belinda glared. "Belittle me all you want but the last laugh will be mine when I dance on your graves."

41

Fargo knew she was trying to get their goat but it got his anyway. "No more talk," he said, and gave her another push.

The solid ground lasted for a quarter of a mile and came to an end at the edge of more swamp.

"Oh, hell," Hosiah said.

"And us without a boat or a canoe," Wayland said.

Fargo counted three gators that he could see. "If there's anything I hate more than a swamp," he said, "it's another swamp."

"We wade out there, we're done for," Wayland said.

"Perhaps we can fool our pursuers into thinking we have," General Canton said, "while we double back to the cabin."

"I'd just as soon shoot the bastards," Wayland said.

"Think, boy, think," Canton said. "Why engage them if we don't have to? Some of us are bound to be hurt, or worse."

Hosiah gestured at Fargo "I'll do what he says. He doesn't rattle easy and we need a clear head to work this out."

Fargo was considering the general's suggestion. With a little luck it could work. "Follow me and step where I step. Keep the woman in the middle. If she tries to bolt, club her."

"I hope she bolts," Wayland said. "I'll club her silly."

Fargo entered the water and waded out until it rose to his knees. Turning, he paralleled the shoreline, moving slowly, alert for alligators and God-knew-what-else. He went about the length of a steamboat when he came to where a thicket edged the swamp. "This will do us." By crouching, he was hidden from the view of anyone who might be following their trail.

"Hunker here in the water?" Wayland said. "I don't know as I like that much."

"Quit your griping," General Canton said. "If you were a soldier in my command, I'd have you cleaning out the stables for a month."

"Maybe you don't care if a gator takes a bite out of your ass but I do," Wayland said.

"That's enough, brother," Hosiah said.

"Not you too?"

Belinda had crouched but was trying to see over the thicket. She started to rise and Fargo pressed the Henry to the side of her neck.

"Don't even think it."

Her eyes were darts of hate.

"Try to warn them and you're the first to die."

Belinda searched his face, and scowled. "I believe you. But don't worry. When my time comes I want it to have meaning."

"Meanin' how?" Wayland said.

"I fight for a cause," Belinda said. "To ensure the South endures forever."

"Nothin' lasts that long, lady."

She fell silent but Fargo didn't trust her. When a twig snapped somewhere above the thicket, he clamped a hand to her mouth and whispered in her ear, "Not a peep."

The others heard it, too. Wayland raised his rifle but Hosiah shook his head.

General Canton tilted his to listen.

Belinda shook with anger but didn't try anything.

Fargo rose up high enough to see stealthy figures gliding from tree to tree. In the lead was Captain Fletcher. Fargo was tempted to shoot but the vegetation didn't allow for a clear shot.

Fletcher and the others stalked on and the opportunity was gone.

Holding firm to Belinda, Fargo moved to the end of the thicket and up a short slope. When Belinda dragged her heels, he roughly jerked her along.

Wayland was grinning like the cat that ate the canary but Fargo wasn't so sure their ruse would work. Fletcher might doubt they'd take to the swamp and backtrack. He started to run.

All went well for a while. They covered a lot of ground. Fargo was anxious to reach the cabin and hunt for the Ovaro. He let go of Belinda but didn't let her stray from his side.

Then Hosiah whispered, "They're after us!" and ducked behind an oak.

Fargo, yanking on Belinda's arm, did the same.

The Southerners were close. "There they are!" one hollered, and they all sought cover.

Captain Fletcher didn't waste any time. "Can you hear me over there?" he yelled.

Not to answer was pointless. "I have ears," Fargo shouted.

"Is it you who's in charge? Or the general?"

General Canton raised his own voice. "I have the final say on matters pertaining to my mission. What do you want?"

"Belinda Montgomery," Captain Fletcher said. "Release her and we'll break this off and let you go."

"And the report you've tried so diligently to get your hands on?" General Canton said.

"She's more important."

"It's a mistake to assume I'd be so stupid," Canton said. "You put the South above all else."

"You're the one making the mistake," Fletcher said. "The report's not worth her life."

"What about your noble cause?"

"Will you or won't you?" Fletcher said.

Fargo was watching Belinda. The look that came over her told him a lot. He saw gratitude, and something else. Something deeper. "I think he's telling the truth."

"Too much is at stake," General Canton said.

"What will it be?" Captain Fletcher shouted. "Belinda? Or your lives?"

The general cupped a hand to his mouth. "Come and take them if you can."

42

A rifle boomed and lead struck the tree Canton was behind.

Fargo pressed the Henry to his shoulder but none of the Southerners showed themselves.

"Stand down!" Captain Fletcher bellowed. "I didn't give the order to fire." He paused. "You might hit Miss Montgomery."

"I'll be damned," General Canton said.

Fargo was thinking of poker. Of how a good bluff won as many hands as holding the best cards. The trick was to know when to bluff and when not to. Good bluffers learned to read the other players. If they were determined to stay in no matter what, then a bluff wouldn't work. "Fletcher," he shouted. "Are you listening?"

"I haven't gone anywhere," was the captain's drawled reply.

"We're leaving and taking Belinda with us. Try to follow and she comes to harm." Fargo was bluffing. He never harmed a woman unless she was out to harm him, and even then he usually went easier on a woman than he would a man.

"You Yankee son of a bitch!" Fletcher yelled.

Belinda suddenly shouted, "Don't listen to him, Jefferson! Do what you have to and don't worry about me."

Fargo grabbed her and covered her mouth. She didn't fight. All she did was stare triumphantly at him over his hand.

Captain Fletcher wasn't long in replying. "All right, scout. A coon knows when it's been treed. Take her and go. But mark me. Harm a hair on her head and there's nowhere on this earth you can hide."

"Who would have thought it?" General Canton said.

Fargo backed away and motioned for the others to do the same. Canton and Hosiah crept after him but Wayland shook his head.

"We should stand and fight. It goes against my nature to tuck tail."

"Tuck it anyway," Hosiah said.

"Our ma would be ashamed of us," Wayland said.

"She'll be more ashamed if you die because you're bein' dumb."

"I'm stayin' and that's final."

"Good idea," Fargo said. "Hold them off as long as you can."

"You don't mind?" Wayland said in some surprise.

"Why should I? Just don't let them kill you too soon. Buy us time to get away."

"That's a hell of a thing to say," Wayland said.

"Take as many of them with you as you can. You won't get them all but do your best."

"It wouldn't bother you a lick if they blew out my wick, would it?"

"If it doesn't bother you, why should it bother me?" Fargo moved on and Canton and Hosiah followed. When next he glanced back, Wayland was running to catch up.

"Thank you," Hosiah whispered.

By now the sun had dipped below the horizon and the gray of twilight rapidly spread. It wouldn't be long before night fell, and they were a long way from the cabin.

General Canton came to Fargo's side. "He's always more active at night, you know."

Fargo didn't need to ask who. "We haven't heard him in a while." Not since that roar earlier.

"He's out there, though. You can bank on it."

Fargo felt so, too.

"Did you notice there are only three men with Fletcher? I shot one by the cabin but what happened to the other?"

"That scream we heard," Fargo guessed.

"Cain has done us a favor and whittled the odds," Canton said. "Could be that's why Fletcher let us leave, Belinda's charms notwithstanding."

"Go to hell," she said.

"We have to find our horses," Fargo mentioned. Their lives might depend on it.

"Ours or theirs is all the same to me," Canton said.

Not to Fargo. He refused to leave Arkansas without the Ovaro. Soon it was too dark to see his hand at arm's length.

The woods came alive with their nightly bedlam. Cries, shrieks, and roars testified to the life-and-death struggles taking place.

Cain Petrie, though, didn't add to the bedlam, which suggested to Fargo that the monster didn't want his presence known. There could be only one reason. Cain was stalking someone. The question was, whom? Them or Fletcher's party?

They were making good time when Belinda cleared her throat. "How about if we strike a deal?"

"Not interested," Fargo said.

"You haven't heard what it is."

"Don't need to," Fargo said. "We're turning you over to the army."

"Who will remand you to civilian custody," General Canton said, "and you'll be put on trial for treason."

"Spend the rest of my days in prison or be hung?" Belinda shook her head. "Neither prospect is appealing."

"Yet you became a spy anyway," Canton said, "and have thrown your life away."

"Sounds to me as if the pot is calling the kettle black," Belinda said. "But it's not over until it's over."

"What can you possibly hope to accomplish? Your friend is dead. Your coconspirators have been foiled."

"You never know," Belinda said.

As if to prove her right, an unearthly roar rocked the woods.

43

Skye Fargo stopped in his tracks. So did the others. In the eerie silence that followed, he swore he heard General Canton swallow.

"He's letting us know he's out there. Letting us know he's hunting us."

Fargo probed the shadows. By his reckoning it would take another twenty minutes to reach the cabin. Plenty of time for the lunatic to strike. "Close up," he said. "Back to back, Belinda in the middle." He waited for them to form a ring around her, then said, "We're going to make a run for it. Keep your position and holler if you spot him."

"I don't want your protection," Belinda said.

"Fine," Wayland said. "Let him rip your head off. I'm tired of your bitchin', anyhow."

"He killed his own sister, remember?" Canton reminded her.

Belinda fell silent.

"On three," Fargo said. He counted, and they broke into motion, matching strides, their shoulders brushing.

"Do you hear that?" Belinda asked, putting her hand on the back of Fargo's buckskin shirt.

Heavy breathing issued from the woods. Cain was making no attempt to hide.

"He'll come at us in a rush," General Canton predicted. "Go for the head or there will be no stopping him."

Fargo remembered Cain's iron arms around him, and how twice the outcast had spared him. He remembered, too, the horror on Eldrida's face as her head was torn from her body.

"There!" Wayland cried, and fired.

The blast made Fargo's ears ring. He sought sign of Petrie and said, "I don't see him."

"He was there, I tell you." Wayland hurriedly reloaded. "I saw him plain as anything."

"Your eyes played tricks," General Canton said.

"I'll prove it to you," Wayland declared, and moved toward the trees.

"No!" Hosiah cried.

Wayland stopped and looked back. "You're worse than Ma. I can take care of myself."

An enormous bulk reared behind the backwoodsman. Fingers as thick as railroad spikes reached for his neck.

"Look out," Fargo shouted.

"Behind you!" Hosiah hollered.

Wayland turned, or tried to. Cain Petrie seized hold and bodily lifted him into the air, shaking him as a terrier might shake a gopher. Wayland's rifle clattered to the ground.

"Damn you!" Wayland cried, trying to kick Cain in the face.

Hosiah darted past Fargo, yelling his brother's name. He aimed his rifle and shouted, "Duck down!"

In an incredible display of strength, Cain hurled Wayland at his brother. Unable to stop or dodge, Hosiah ran headlong into him. The pair tumbled, Hosiah getting the worst of it.

Cain moved to finish them off.

"Try me," Fargo cried. He fired but Cain kept coming. He fired again and Cain charged faster and he fired a third time as Cain plowed into him and he was sent flying. He crashed into a tree, fell, and lay unable to move. He tried, but the best he could do was raise an arm. His back was to the others. He heard Belinda scream, heard blows and shots and another roar from Cain Petrie.

Then silence.

Gritting his teeth, Fargo managed to make it to his knees.

General Canton lay on his back, and wasn't moving. Hosiah was doubled over, his head bowed, blood darkening his cheek. Wayland, like Fargo, had been flung a good distance and was shakily attempting to stand.

Belinda was nowhere to be seen.

Fargo swore. The Henry was by his boot and he picked it up and used it to prop himself up as he rose and moved to Canton. The general had been struck on the ear and it was split and bleeding. Fargo shook him but all Canton did was groan. He shook harder, saying, "General? Snap out of it."

Canton opened his eyes. Licking his lips, he asked, "Is my head still attached?"

"Seems to be," Fargo said.

"That explains the pain."

"It took her," Hosiah said. "The critter swooped her into its arms and ran off with her."

Fargo remembered being told that the Night Terror never attacked women. Not anymore. First Eldrida and now Belinda.

"I shot him," Wayland said. "Smack in the chest but it had no effect. That thing ain't human."

"We all shot him," General Canton said.

"How is it that critter ain't dead then?" Hosiah asked.

"My guess?" Canton replied while rising onto his elbows. "He's so big, he absorbs lead like a sponge. And he doesn't seem to feel pain. I've heard of people like that. There's a name for their condition but it eludes me. Maybe it has something to do with the aberration of his birth."

"Aber-what?" Wayland said.

"He's a freak of nature."

"No foolin'," Wayland said.

"We have to go after him," Fargo told them.

Out of the darkness stepped Captain Jefferson Fletcher and his fellow secessionists, their rifles leveled.

"You're not going anywhere, mister," Fletcher said.

44

"Raise your hands where we can see them," Captain Fletcher commanded, "or suffer the consequences."

"No," Fargo said.

"We'll shoot if you force us."

"You do," Fargo said, "and Belinda is as good as dead. Or don't you care as much as you claimed?"

Fletcher glanced around. "We heard her scream and the shots. Where—?"

"He took her," Fargo said.

"*It* took her," Wayland amended. "The critter."

"That thing she told me about? The creature that ripped the head off of one of my men? *It* has Belinda?"

"Afraid so," Fargo said.

"I saw its tracks," Fletcher said, aghast.

"With my own eyes I saw him rip the head off his sister," Fargo said. "He'll do the same to Belinda. It's only a matter of time."

"Good God," Fletcher breathed.

"Together, we might be able to stop him and save her."

"Join forces?"

One of Fletcher's men said, "Hold on. What about that secret Yankee report? Isn't that more important?"

Fletcher hesitated.

"Credit me with some intelligence," General Canton said. "I'm not stupid enough to have it on me. It was on my horse, which the lunatic scared off. By the time we find it, your lady friend will have met a horrible end."

"You have a choice to make," Fargo said to the captain. "That damned report or the woman."

From out of the night to the south wafted a scream of mortal terror. It galvanized Captain Fletcher into taking several steps and exclaiming, "Belinda! No!"

"Make up your mind, damn it," Fargo said. The woman was his enemy and would have killed him but he couldn't just leave her to suffer at Cain Petrie's gruesome hands.

"I urge haste as well," General Canton said. "The brute is temperamental. He might let her live a while. Long enough for us to find them."

"It won't be pretty if that critter yanks off her noggin," Wayland contributed.

"Belinda," Fletcher said again. His men were looking at him with uncertainty, awaiting his orders.

"I propose a truce, Captain," General Canton said. "We set aside our differences and go after her. Her life matters more than our political loyalties, or don't you agree?"

"She means a lot to me," Fletcher said. His tone implied she meant considerably more.

"Then do we or don't we?" Canton offered his hand. "If we have a truce, let's shake on it and quit wasting precious time."

Captain Fletcher stared at the general's hand, then went over and clasped it. "We have a truce."

Canton looked at Fletcher's men. "All hostilities are to cease until Miss Montgomery is found. Agreed, gentlemen? A nod will suffice."

They all nodded.

"Excellent," General Canton said.

Fargo helped Hosiah to stand. They found his rifle and Canton gave him a handkerchief to stanch his split cheek.

Captain Fletcher was staring forlornly to the south. "How will we find her in the dark? I can't track at night. No one can."

"Torches," Fargo said. "Quickly."

Fletcher snapped commands and his men hustled to find suitable limbs. Setting his rifle down, he took off his shirt, drew a knife, and commenced to cut off the sleeves.

Fargo, meanwhile, kindled a small fire.

When the Southerners returned, Fletcher wrapped a strip from his shirt around an end of each broken branch and tied the strips fast. He gave the branches to Fargo, who held them to the fire and passed a torch to General Canton and Wayland and Fletcher and saved the last for himself.

"This person or whatever it is that took her," Fletcher said. "He'll see our torches and know we're after him."

"We want him to," Fargo said. "It'll take his mind off her. Maybe keep her alive a little longer."

"I pray you're right."

"One thing before we start," General Canton said. "When it

attacks us, and it will, have your men go for the head. We've put enough lead into it to sink a ship and it's as strong and fast as ever."

"You heard him," Fletcher said.

"Life sure is strange," a lanky Southerner remarked. "One minute we're out to spill their blood and now we're out to spill something else's."

"Whatever took Miss Montgomery, the eight of us will make gator bait of it," another confidently predicted.

"Provided," General Canton said, "it doesn't make gator bait of us first."

45

Fargo and Fletcher assumed the lead. They were the best trackers. In the combined light of their flickering torches, Cain Petrie's trail was as plain as a bull buffalo's. As usual, Cain had plowed through everything in his path. Thickets, thorns, pools where gators might lurk, nothing stopped him.

"What kind of man are we after?" Captain Fletcher asked in wonder as they skirted water where the glowing eyes of alligators stared back at them. "He's not scared of anything."

"He's more animal than man," Fargo said.

"Will he . . ." Fletcher stopped. "That is, do you think he'll lay his hands . . ." He stopped again.

"Will he rape her?"

"That's my fear."

"I don't know," Fargo said. "He hasn't shown much interest in women that way. Maybe he's curious."

"Or wants a mate," Fletcher said.

"There's that," Fargo conceded.

The trail led ever deeper into the swamp. Again and again they had to detour around bogs and deep pools and tangles. It slowed them.

Twice they had to stop to make new torches. That slowed them, too.

Mosquitoes and other insects were a plague. Gators and snakes were a constant menace. They slogged through terrain that would tire an ox but no one complained.

They were thinking of the woman, and of her fate should they fail.

About four in the morning Fargo called a halt on a patch of solid ground. "We'll rest a bit."

"I'm not tired," Captain Fletcher said.

"They are," Fargo replied, with a bob of his head at the weary Southerners, who were gratefully sitting or lying down.

"I should go on ahead," Fletcher said.

"Not by your lonesome."

"We've known each other for over a year now. I've been thinking of asking for her hand in marriage but the time never seemed to be right."

"You can ask her once she's safe."

Fletcher didn't seem to hear him. "I'll never forgive myself if she comes to harm. I shouldn't have let you take her."

"Flogging yourself won't help."

A loud splash made them jump. The water that fringed the hummock rippled and lapped.

"An alligator," General Canton said.

If Fargo never saw another gator his whole life long, he'd be a happy man. Give him coyotes and wolves and elk any day.

"You're a good tracker," Fletcher remarked. "Better than I am, I think."

"Lots of practice," Fargo said.

"You don't sound like a Yankee but I have to ask. Which side will you take when war breaks out?"

"My own."

"That's no answer. You'll have to pick one or the other. Everyone will. All because the North is on their high horse about owning slaves."

"I don't own any."

"Me either. But I'll fight for the right of those who do want to own them. Whenever a government says that someone can't do this or that, it's tyranny."

"I heard that," General Canton spoke up. "And I disagree. I'm from the South, too, but I don't believe that anyone has the right to own another human being."

"That's enough," Fargo said, "from both of you."

"I beg your pardon?" Canton said.

"We have a truce, remember? Until we find Belinda, forget about the war. We'll get along better."

"I see. You're worried we'll come to blows."

"What I want to know," Wayland said, "is how long we'll keep at this? We don't have food or drinkin' water."

"As long as it takes," Fargo said.

A swath of crushed brush and broken branches brought them to a new expanse of swamp. Dawn wasn't far off. Fewer gators bellowed. Fewer frogs croaked. The nightlife was winding down.

"We're so far in," Captain Fletcher remarked, "I doubt another human being has ever set foot here."

"Cain Petrie has," Fargo said.

"But he ain't human," Wayland said.

"What else would he be?" Canton said.

"I don't hardly know," Wayland replied. "Sure, he had a ma and pa, like the rest of us. What popped out of her womb, though, weren't like you or me. My grandma would say he's a demon out of hell."

"That's ridiculous."

"You call it human when he's been shot eight or ten times and doesn't die? You call it human when he lives with gators and snakes and ain't ever been eaten or bit? You call it human that he never tires?"

"You're making more out of him than there is."

"I ain't hardly made enough," Wayland said.

Fargo had noticed that the trail they were following, if drawn on a map, would run in a straight line. It suggested Cain wasn't roaming at random, that he was making a beeline for a specific spot. He mentioned it to the others.

"Perhaps it's where his father had him dumped," General Canton speculated. "Where he lived all those years, until recently."

Dawn broke, painting the eastern sky pink and red and yellow. Hour by hour the sun rose higher. So did the temperature.

"I see what you mean about this thing never tiring," Captain Fletcher said to Wayland. "He goes on and on forever."

"All that energy," Wayland said. "He's like a bunny I used to have."

The other man looked at him.

"When I was a sprout," Wayland said. "I had him for a pet for a while and then we ate him."

The sun was directly overhead when they emerged from a cypress grove. Fargo, out in front, stopped so suddenly that Captain Fletcher walked into him.

"What—?" Fletcher said, and his mouth fell.

Ahead was an old estate. Willows covered the eastern third and grass much of the rest. In the middle, green with moss and decrepit with age, reared a three-story structure. In its prime it must have been a fine mansion but now it was on the verge of collapse. Many of the windows were broken. Those that weren't were coated thick with mold and dust. Vines entwined the porch posts and a section of rail had rotted and fallen.

"What in hell?" Hosiah blurted.

"A house way out here?" Wayland said.

"I wonder," General Canton said, thoughtfully rubbing his chin.

"Let's hear it," Fargo said.

"The Petrie family was rich once, yes? Or so we were told. It could be that the father had this built to get away to now and then. A home away from home, if you will. Or perhaps he used it for hunting and fishing, as he later did the lodge."

"But why abandon it?" Captain Fletcher asked. "Why not sell it if the upkeep became too much?"

Canton snapped his fingers as if an idea had occurred to him. "Eldrida Petrie told us that her father had Cain taken off into the swamp and left to fend for himself. Remember? We wondered how a father could do that to his son." Canton indicated the run-down mansion. "This might be the answer. Petrie didn't have Cain dropped in the swamp. He had him brought here. Where Cain at least stood a chance to survive."

"I'll be damned," Fargo said. It made perfect sense.

"Maybe the parents hired someone to look after him," Canton continued, "but somehow or other Cain wound up on his own. He's been here all this time, and only recently ventured beyond the swamp."

"And started killin' folks," Wayland said.

"He must be in there right this minute," Captain Fletcher said. "Belinda, too." He took a step.

"Hold on," Fargo said. "We stay together. Numbers are the only edge we have."

"Then why are we still standing here? Belinda is in there, I tell you."

The next instant, from out of the bowels of the mansion, came a woman's scream.

46

Captain Jefferson Fletcher shouted, "I'm coming, Belinda!" And off he charged.

"Hell," Fargo said, chasing after him. To go bursting in was reckless. Cain could be anywhere and knew the inside of the mansion better than they did. "Wait for us!"

Fletcher had no intention of stopping. He reached the steps and bounded up. Without warning, the fourth step cracked and buckled. His leg went in a hole clear to his hip. He tried to pull it out but it was stuck fast.

Fargo reached him. "Let me help." He pulled but the leg wouldn't budge.

"It's caught fast," Fletcher said. "Something is pressing against my ankle."

By then the others were there.

"So long as there ain't any black widows or rattlers in that hole you should be all right," Wayland said.

"Forget about me," Fletcher snapped, struggling furiously. "Go help her."

"My friends and I will go," Fargo said. "Your men will get you free." He was up the steps before anyone could argue. He crossed to a decayed door covered with moss that hung by one hinge. He pushed it so he could slip past and it creaked and swayed. Suddenly the hinge gave way. Fargo sprang back as the door crashed down.

The thud seemed to reverberate throughout the mansion.

"That critter will know we're here now," Wayland said.

"He probably already does," General Canton said.

Fargo warily stepped into a spacious foyer hung thick with spider webs. A moldy scent made him want to cough.

Aged draperies sagged over the windows. One rod had shattered and the drapes lay in a dusty pile on the floor. A chandelier that once must have glittered and sparkled was now so caked with dust that its facets were dulled. A carpet had long since been reduced to tatters while the rest of the floor was inches thick with dust and leaves that had blown in and other bits of debris.

"I'd warrant that Cain is the only one who has lived here for a very long time," General Canton remarked.

Petrie's footprints were everywhere. It helped explain how Cain had survived for so long. In here he was safe from the gators and snakes and quicksand. He had to venture out only for food.

"Which way?" Wayland whispered.

Dark and gloomy halls branched off into the depths. To their right, wide stairs curved up to the second floor.

"I say we split up," General Canton suggested.

"It would be a mistake," Fargo said.

"We'll find her faster, and isn't that the point?"

Faint weeping fell on their ears. It was clearly a woman. But it wasn't clear where the sound came from. It might be down any of the halls or even upstairs.

"Hell," Hosiah said. "Where is she?"

"We separate," General Canton said with finality. He was accustomed to giving orders and being obeyed and didn't wait for them to object. Squaring his shoulders, he strode into a hall.

Wayland swore and took another, Hosiah the last.

That left upstairs.

Every stair creaked no matter how lightly Fargo tread. At the landing he stopped. He had his choice of two murky hallways.

Swiping at a cobweb, Fargo recoiled when a large spider skittered from his hand and up into a recess. He'd never seen a spider so huge. Fitting, he supposed, that it lived there.

Swallowing to wet his dry mouth, Fargo advanced. It wasn't just Cain and the spiders he had to worry about. The floor might give way as the step outside had. He could feel how weak the boards were; many sagged under his weight.

He came to an open door. The room was black as pitch. He poked his head in, saw nothing but the blackness, and drew back. Cobwebs clung to his hat.

He wished they still had their torches. He thought about making one, should he find the means.

The next room wasn't as dark. Sunlight streamed in a dusty window. The curtains that once covered it were in shambles. A four-poster bed sat against one wall, a dresser against another. The bed sagged and the canopy was fit to collapse.

Fargo moved on.

The next room was a revelation. A crib was in a corner, a bassinet on a table. Toys littered the floor. An old rattle here, a wooden horse there. Cain's footprints were everywhere. Blankets had been piled in another corner, and from the impression in them, it was apparent Cain slept in this room often.

This had been Cain's when he was small.

Fargo wondered how much the man-brute remembered of his life back then. Evidently enough that this room was special to him.

He was about to continue searching when shouts rose from the foyer.

"Fargo! Canton! Where are you?"

Captain Fletcher had been freed. He and his men were standing uncertainly before the dark hallways when Fargo appeared at the landing.

"Any sign of her?" Captain Fletcher asked.

"Not up here."

Fletcher grunted and turned to his men. "Vernon, take the right corridor. Royd, the left. Leland, come with me down this middle one."

"Wait for me," Fargo said. He was wasting his time upstairs. Cain and the pretty spy weren't there.

But Fletcher didn't. He gestured at his men and they hurried off.

"Wait," Fargo said again, but when he reached the bottom he was alone. He moved to the hall Fletcher took and whispered the captain's name but got no answer.

Against his better judgment, Fargo followed. He hadn't gone far when a puff of cool air let him know the hall forked.

The place was a maze. Fargo realized it would be easy to get turned around and lost. He groped his way into the new hall and almost immediately his boot bumped something that clattered.

Fargo hoped Cain hadn't heard. He took a long step over whatever he had bumped. Cautiously edging forward, he couldn't help thinking they were mice to Cain Petrie's cat, in the cat's very lair.

His boot bumped something else. Something that yielded and felt suspiciously familiar. Squatting, he tentatively ran a hand over it to see if he was right.

He was.

He'd found a body.

47

A hasty examination revealed two things. First, the man was one of Fletcher's. The only one to wear suspenders. Second, his head had been bent at an angle no head should be bent.

Cain's work, obviously.

Fargo rose, his Henry at his waist. He listened for heavy breathing.

Suddenly a gun boomed. Four shots, followed by a hideous roar and then a screech of agony.

Fargo had the impression the shots and the cry came from under him. He resisted an urge to rush blindly on.

By now his eyes had adjusted enough that he could distinguish vague outlines. It didn't help much.

More cool air fanned his face. Dank air, as from subterranean depths.

A yawning cavity appeared. Another flight of stairs, only these led down instead of up.

Fargo took a step and his foot clanked. Puzzled, he crouched and discovered the steps were made of metal, not wood. He took another step, as lightly as possible, and the metal groaned.

Fargo backed away. To descend quietly was impossible. He needed another way down.

From somewhere below came a growl.

Fargo tensed.

Heavy feet thumped on the metal stairs. More groaning echoed, the metal under great stress.

Cain was climbing toward him.

Whirling, Fargo ran. In the dark he was no match for the giant. The prudent thing was to find somewhere to make a stand. A doorway on his left offered haven. He pushed on the door and it grated open wide enough for him to slip inside. There was no window. Just more infernal blackness. Putting his back to a wall, he pointed his rifle at the door.

Loud breathing filled the hall. Feet scraped in that peculiar gait Cain Petrie had, and he sniffed a few times.

Fargo wondered if the madman could smell him. If so, he'd be cornered in a windowless room.

The scraping neared the door. Suddenly it stopped. Cain was right outside.

Fargo waited for him to appear. His only hope was to go for the head and fire as fast as he could.

The hall was quiet.

Fargo's nerves were on the verge of exploding. He strained his eyes, his ears.

He figured Cain knew he was in there and was waiting for him to give himself away.

Shouts rose from below, Belinda yelling, "Help me! I'm down here! Someone! Anyone! Please!"

A grunt sounded, and there was the swift *thump-thump-thump* of Cain Petrie moving off.

Fargo darted to the doorway. He was averse to back-shooting but in Petrie's case he'd make an exception. Anything to end the killing.

The monster had already reached the stairs and was noisily rushing down.

About to go help Belinda, Fargo stiffened on hearing footsteps behind him.

"Who's there?" a voice demanded. "I know someone is."

"Canton?" Fargo said.

The general came up. "Fargo? Thank God. I've been wandering all over, trying to get my bearings."

"Same here."

"You were right," the general said. "We never should have separated."

"One of Fletcher's men is dead."

"I know."

"There's a basement," Fargo said. "Cain has Belinda down there."

"At least she's still alive."

"Follow me." Fargo turned to the stairs.

"Not so fast," Canton said. "We should find something to light our way instead of floundering in this darkness."

"I couldn't agree more," Fargo told him.

They retraced their way down the hall. Fargo stepped over the body but Canton didn't lift his leg high enough and tripped and almost fell.

"Damn me," he said.

Soon they came to a junction.

"I don't remember this," Fargo said. Yet they couldn't have taken a wrong turn. Or could they?

Fargo turned right, thinking it would take them to rooms with windows. After a short distance he stopped.

"What is it?" Canton whispered.

"Listen."

From ahead came slithering sounds, as of something moving along the floor.

"What the hell?" General Canton said. "A snake, do you think? Or, God help us, possibly an alligator?"

"How would a gator get in the house?"

"You said there's a basement. Maybe it opens onto the swamp."

Whatever it was, it was slithering toward them.

"I can't tell you how much I hate this," General Canton whispered. "I say we beat a prudent retreat and find another way."

Fargo was more than willing. But as they were about to get out of there, the slithering stopped and there was a hoarse cry.

"Help me!"

"It's Hosiah Wilkes!" Canton exclaimed.

A few bounds brought Fargo to a form lying in the middle of the hall. He crouched and gripped a hand that weakly rose to his. "We're here," he said. "The general and me."

Hosiah coughed violently. "Can't hardly breathe," he gasped.

Carefully shifting him onto his back, Fargo rested Hosiah's head on his boot. "Cain Petrie?"

"He came out of nowhere," Hosiah said. "Grabbed me and squeezed before I could so much as holler. I blacked out and just came to a bit ago."

"How bad is it?" General Canton asked.

"I'm busted up inside," Hosiah said.

"Don't worry," Canton said. "We'll take you out of here and one of us will tend you."

"No need to go to all that bother."

"Why not?"

"I'm just about dead," Hosiah said.

48

Fargo put a hand to Hosiah's chest and Hosiah writhed and said, "Don't."

"What can we do for you?" General Canton asked.

"Find my brother," Hosiah said. "Don't let the thing get him, too." He coughed and shook and looked up at Fargo. "For what it's worth, you'd do to ride the river with."

"I'll find Wayland," Fargo said.

"Tell him to break the news easy to our ma. Losin' Abimelech and me will cause her a heap of sorrow."

"Damn that lunatic, anyhow," General Canton said.

Hosiah closed his eyes and deflated as if all the air had escaped from his lungs. His next-to-last words were, "Never reckoned to go this way. An eye for an eye can cost more than the eye is worth."

"Eloquently phrased, sir," Canton said.

"Elo-what?" Hosiah said, and died.

"Hell," Canton said. "We didn't hit it off at first but he proved to be a good man in a pinch."

Fargo laid Hosiah's head on the floor and closed his eyes. He felt at Hosiah's waist but his revolver and knife were gone. A pouch was across his chest, and when Fargo opened it, he found a godsend. "Lucifers," he let the general know.

"What do we use for the torch?"

They went from room to room. In the third was another four-poster bed. Fargo was set to rip the canopy off and break a post when the general walked over holding a lamp.

"Look at this. When I shake it, it sounds half full."

Fargo took it and smelled the wick. "Whale oil." The odor was like no other.

The wick lit on the third try. The flame was tiny but it would do. Raising the lamp over his head, Fargo headed for the metal stairs. "Time to end this."

"Before I forget, if anything should happen to me, remember what I told you. The troop report is in my bedroll."

"Which is on your horse," Fargo recollected. "Which was scared off and could be anywhere."

"Your horse was scared off too."

Fargo didn't need to be reminded. He'd been worried about the Ovaro ever since.

Thanks to the lamp, they reached the stairs in half the time. At the top they stopped and leaned over the metal banister. It was like peering into a well. The glow from their lamp didn't radiate far enough down to show what was below.

"Into the lion's den we shall go," General Canton said.

"Watch out for the lion."

At the bottom lay another of Fletcher's men, horribly mangled.

"Only Captain Fletcher and one other left," Canton said.

"Plus Wayland."

Rusted tools hung on the walls and there was a workbench that hadn't seen use in decades. At both ends of the chamber were doorways.

"Should you take right and I take left?" Canton proposed.

"You want to make the same mistake twice?"

"No," Canton said. "I don't."

Fargo went right. Something crunched underfoot and he looked down to find the floor littered with bones. Scores and scores, mostly small animals, raccoons and possums, as well as an astonishing number of rats and mice.

"I can't say much for his diet," Canton said.

The doorway was so narrow, Fargo wondered how Cain could fit through it.

He raised the lamp high again and was jolted by the sight of Belinda hanging on a wall. Spikes had been driven through her wrists and ankles. Under her lay Captain Fletcher, drops of her blood mixed with his from a gash on his head.

"Merciful heaven," General Canton said, and ran over.

Fargo exercised more caution. He saw another body and nudged it with his foot. The face that flopped with lifeless eyes was the last of Fletcher's men.

Canton was rolling Fletcher over. The captain moaned and Canton said excitedly, "He's alive, thank God!" Canton shook him. "Captain Fletcher? Can you hear me, man? We must get you on your feet."

Fletcher opened his eyes and looked about in dread, then clutched the general's shirt. "Look out!" he said. "He's here."

159

"Calm down. We haven't see him," Canton said. "He must have gone off somewhere."

Cain Petrie roared.

Fargo spun just as the behemoth hurtled out of the shadows. General Canton tried to stand but Petrie slammed into him and Canton cartwheeled.

Fargo set down the lamp to free his hands to shoot. He was straightening when it felt as if a rampaging longhorn smashed into his side. He tumbled boots over hat and crashed down on his belly. He sought to rise but the chamber was swimming. Worse, he'd lost the Henry.

Cain Petrie spread his arms and roared. He flew at Captain Fletcher, who had propped himself against the wall under Belinda and was fumbling with his revolver.

Seizing Fletcher by the wrist, Cain wrenched. Fletcher cried out and dropped his six-gun, and Cain wrapped a hand around his neck.

By then Fargo had his Colt out. He fired square into the middle of Cain's broad back, thumbed the hammer, fired again. Cain Petrie howled. Letting go of Fletcher, he turned and growled.

"Die, you son of a bitch." Fargo would kill him if it was the last thing he did.

He aimed at Cain's chest, at where the heart should be. One shot and it would be over. But Cain was on him before he could shoot, driving a huge fist into Fargo's gut.

Never, ever, did a punch cause Fargo so much hurt. His consciousness was sucked into a void and spewed out again. He sprawled to his hands and knees.

General Canton was on his feet and had drawn his revolver. He took deliberate aim, saying, "I've got you now."

Cain turned and leaped. Only legs as thick and powerful as his could have propelled him that far. Canton's revolver went off when Cain was in midair. Then the giant struck. The general flew like a rag doll and Cain crouched, unscathed.

Captain Fletcher, on his side on the floor, fired. He was holding his Smith & Wesson two-handed to steady his aim.

Cain Petrie reacted as if he had been punched. It didn't slow him, though, didn't lessen the ferocity of his retribution. He swatted the six-shooter from Fletcher's grasp and pummeled the captain with his sledgehammer fists.

"Leave him be, you animal!" Belinda wailed. Despite the spikes in her limbs, despite the torment she must be enduring, she thought only of Fletcher.

Fargo struggled to stand but his legs wouldn't work. Bile rose in his gorge and he swallowed it.

"Jefferson, can you hear me?" Belinda cried.

No, Fletcher couldn't, but Cain certainly could. He straightened and stood before her, cocking his grotesque head from side to side.

"I wish you were dead!" Belinda shrieked.

Cain Petrie put a hand on each side of her head. Belinda twisted and squirmed and then screamed and went on screaming.

With an ease that defied belief, the hulking behemoth tore her head from her neck. Not quickly, as he had with the others, but slowly.

Fargo heard her tendons pop, heard the rip of her skin. He tried—God, he tried—to get up and help her but his body refused to cooperate. For as long as he lived, he'd never forget her death wail.

"Noooooo!" Captain Fletcher was up and had his revolver but in his fury over Belinda he began beating Cain instead of shooting him.

Cain hardly seemed to notice. He was holding Belinda's head in his hand, her blood and gore smeared on his fingers. He looked at Fletcher, and at Belinda's head, and drove her head into Fletcher's face. Once, twice, yet again, and Fletcher tottered.

"Belinda!" the captain croaked, her hair and some of her flesh stuck to his pulped lips.

Cain's next blow drove Belinda's head so far into Fletcher's face that when Cain let go, Fletcher's face and hers were stuck together. Fletcher took a single step and collapsed, the two heads hitting the floor as one.

Fargo saw his Colt. He grabbed it, cocked it, and rose to his knees.

Cain was staring at his ghastly handiwork, fascinated by the two-heads-in-one.

He didn't notice when Fargo took aim. At the blast he swung around and bared his teeth.

General Canton charged into the light, shooting as he came. Scarlet misted from Cain's neck and chest. It wasn't enough, though. Cain reached Canton in a long leap and ripped the general's arm from his body.

Canton looked numbly at Fargo and mouthed words Fargo couldn't hear. He tried to back away but Cain beat him with his own arm. The blows brought the general to his knees.

Fargo resorted to a desperate gambit. He willed his legs to work and lurched at Cain and thrust the Colt's muzzle in Cain's deformed ear. He fired once, twice. That should have done it but Cain stayed upright and his fist was an anvil.

The floor swept at Fargo. He drifted on tides of the faintest awareness until shaking brought him around. A hand was on his shoulder.

"Don't you die on me, damn you. You're the only one still breathin'."

Fargo opened his eyes. "I am?"

"We wouldn't be talkin' if you weren't," Wayland Wilkes said. He gazed about the chamber in stunned dismay. "They're dead. Every last one of them."

Fargo turned his head, and recoiled. Cain's face wasn't an arm's length away, that hideous visage made more so by the contortions of his last breath.

"It's all right," Wayland said. "Ugly is dead too." He paused and bowed his head. "I would have been here sooner but I found my brother."

"I'm sorry," Fargo said.

"Two I've lost," Wayland said. "There's just me now." He shook himself, and slid a hand under Fargo's arm. "Let's get the hell out of here. What do you say?"

It took an hour to find their way, another half an hour to dig a grave for Hosiah. The rest of the bodies Fargo left in the mansion. Eventually it would collapse and bury what was left of their bones.

The rest of the day was spent in reaching the cabin. They were still a ways off when a whinny brought a smile to Fargo's lips and out of the woods trotted the Ovaro. He draped his arm over its neck and patted it and for the first time in days was content.

Wayland helped him dispose of Adelade and the Southerner the general had shot, and the next morning they went horse hunting. They didn't find Wayland's mount but they did find Hosiah's.

They didn't find the general's horse, either.

Fargo spent two more days searching. He scoured every square acre for a mile around and found Adelade's animal with its reins caught.

But there was still no sign of the general's.

Although Wayland was eager to return home, he agreed to help hunt one last day. They started at the crack of dawn and it was ten or so when Wayland came across hoofprints and hollered.

Fargo had no trouble following them. He was so intent on the tracks that he almost made a fatal blunder.

"Look out!" Wayland hollered. "You're ridin' into quicksand."

Fargo drew sharp rein. "I'm obliged." He had to look close to tell it wasn't solid ground.

"This don't mean what I think it means, does it?" Wayland asked.

"Let's find out." Fargo circled, seeking evidence the horse had made it out. When they had gone completely around, he again drew rein and said, "I'll be damned."

"Do you reckon it was the general's?"

"The way things have gone," Fargo said, "it wouldn't surprise me."

"What will you do now?"

"Ride to New Orleans and get word to the army. Then head west where I belong." Fargo smiled. "After a few nights of cards and painted ladies and drinking whiskey until it comes out my ears."

"I like that last part," Wayland Wilkes said.

The Rocky Mountains, 1861—two towns
wage war and Fargo is caught in the middle.

Skye Fargo wasn't expecting trouble. He was high in the Rocky Mountains, camped for the night in a small clearing. His fire had died low and the Ovaro was dozing. He lay on his back with his head propped in his hands and listened to the wavering howl of a far-off wolf.

A big man, broader at the shoulders than most, Fargo wore buckskins and a red bandanna and boots. Unlike some men, he never took his boots off when he turned in for the night. Not in the wilds. A man never knew but when danger might threaten.

Fargo was on the cusp of drifting off when the Ovaro raised its head and nickered. Instantly, he was alert. The stallion was staring toward the rutted road they had been following for the better part of three days. Its ears were pricked and its nostrils flared, and it stamped a front hoof.

Fargo rolled off his blankets and into a crouch, drawing his Colt as he rose. It was pushing midnight. No ordinary traveler would be abroad that late. Only those up to no good.

Working quickly, using his saddlebags and a branch he'd broken for firewood, Fargo rigged his blanket so at a glance it would appear he was asleep. As a last touch he placed his hat where his head would have been.

Melting into the shadows, Fargo waited. It could have been hostiles. The Utes weren't happy about having their territory overrun by the white man. Or it could have been highwaymen. Thanks to all the gold and silver strikes that were luring pilgrims by the thousands to the mountains, outlaws were as thick as fleas on a hound dog.

Fargo heard footfalls and a whisper. They were clumsy about it. That told him they weren't Utes. No self-respecting warrior would have been so careless. By the sounds he counted three.

Fargo had crouched in front of a small pine so his silhouette would blend into the tree's. They didn't spot him. They were intent on his blankets. At the edge of the clearing they stopped, and to Fargo's amusement, one of them was dumb enough to whisper to the others.

"Do you reckon it's him?"

"Has to be. Look at that horse. If that ain't a pinto, I'll eat my spurs."

Fargo's amusement faded. The Ovaro wasn't a pinto but those who didn't know horses often mistook it for one. Of more interest was the fact that these three lunkheads were after him, specifically. Few people knew he was in that part of the country at that particular time. His mind raced with what it might mean. He had questions, and he wanted answers.

The third man whispered something Fargo didn't catch and the three spread out and converged. Their pistols were out and pointed but they weren't very sure of themselves. They inched forward as if treading on eggshells.

Fargo's natural inclination was to gun them then and there. Instead he said, "That's far enough, gents."

Two froze but the third spun and raised his revolver. Fargo fanned the Colt and the slug caught the would-be assassin in the chest and smashed him onto his back.

The other two stared as their companion writhed and gurgled and died.

"Are you as stupid as your pard?" Fargo said. "Drop your hardware or the same happens to you."

One man dropped his as if it were a hot coal. "Don't shoot, mister. Please. I ain't hankerin' to die."

The last outlaw hesitated. "You'll kill us anyway."

"Not if you shed that six-shooter," Fargo said.

"I don't believe you."

"Your choice."

The man made up his mind. He dived and fired at where he thought Fargo must have been but he was wide by a yard. Fargo fanned the Colt twice and the body flopped a few times and was still.

"God Almighty!" the man who had dropped his revolver exclaimed, and jerked his arms at the stars. "Please, mister. I have a missus and five sprouts."

Fargo unfurled and warily walked over.

The surviving specimen was in his twenties. He was cockeyed and had a nose that had been busted once and was bent at an odd angle. Tufts of hair grew from his cheeks and chin, and his mouth was crooked. He was scrawny, besides, and by the look of things, hadn't made the acquaintance of water and soap in years.

"*You* have a wife?" Fargo said.

"I sure do. Her name is"—he paused for almost five seconds— "Clementine. And don't forget our five young'uns. There's, uh, Sally and Chester and, uh, Penelope, and, uh, the other two."

"As a liar you're downright pitiful."

"What makes you think I ain't tellin' the truth?"

Fargo sniffed.

"Oh. Well, it could be my missus doesn't mind stink. Some females don't use their noses much."

"Do you ever listen to yourself?"

"What?"

"How about I if shoot you in the leg?" Fargo said. "Will you still claim you're married?"

"I'd get a divorce right quick."

Fargo smothered a grin. This assassin was about as intimidating as a kitten. "What's your handle?"